MW01146923

PURRFECT TRAP

THE MYSTERIES OF MAX 15

NIC SAINT

PUSS IN PRINT PUBLICATIONS

PURRFECT TRAP

The Mysteries of Max 15

Copyright © 2019 by Nic Saint

Edited by Chereese Graves

www.nicsaint.com

Give feedback on the book at: info@nicsaint.com

facebook.com/nicsaintauthor
@nicsaintauthor

First Edition

Printed in the U.S.A

PROLOGUE

*H*eavy rain lashed the windows of the homes that lined the road. A storm had blown in overnight and the wind had picked up speed. Lightning slashed the sky and the night was black as ink. Elon Pope, as he pushed down on the pedals of his bicycle, cursed his decision to take his bike and not the Lambo. He could have been home by now, warm and dry, heating himself by the family fireplace. But no, he had to play the hero again.

When his sister Marcie had accused him of being a climate denier and a grade-A polluter, he'd pointed out to her that he wasn't merely the proud owner of a Maserati and a Lamborghini but also of a good old-fashioned bike, so when she'd challenged him to hit the pubs on his bike and leave his supercars at home, he'd foolishly taken her on.

And now here he was, riding along this deserted stretch of road in the middle of the night, while Hampton Covians were all safely tucked into their beds, pedaling away like a madman. His nice Moreschi shoes were ruined, his black Armani jeans spattered and caked with mud and muck, and his favorite Ralph Lauren polo shirt completely soaked.

His hair was plastered to his skull and he had trouble seeing which way he was going from the rain lashing his face and running into his eyes. Oh, damn you, Marcie.

Soon he'd left Hampton Cove behind, and was traveling along one of the smaller roads out of town. No posh residences here, though—only a bunch of old houses and rundown farms. One of those old houses was his family home, and the knowledge that he was close made him push down on those pedals with renewed fervor. One more mile.

And he'd just reached a fork in the road, and taken a left turn, when suddenly lightning flashed once again, only this time hitting much closer. It actually struck a willow tree close by and the sparks made Elon utter an inadvertent yelp of fear.

Yikes. This horrible storm was not only inconvenient but also seriously dangerous! Hadn't he once read about a man being struck by lightning in just such a storm? And what had the advice been? To hide under a tree? Or not to hide under a tree? He couldn't remember. One thing he shouldn't do was stand still in the middle of the street. Or ride an iron bicycle on the open road… He looked around for a moment, wondering whether to go on or to take cover for a moment. Maybe let the worst of the storm blow over.

He wiped the rain from his eyes and glanced over to the old Buschmann house, just beyond the bend. Rumor had it that the place was haunted by the ghost of old Royce Buschmann. Nonsense, of course. Old man Buschmann had simply died and the house had fallen into disrepair, its owner having had no children or siblings to inherit the place.

Lightning struck once more, eerily illuminating the old structure. He shivered, and not just from being soaked through and through. It was almost as if the house had a soul. As if an evil entity possessed it. Even as a child he'd never been able to pass the house without a shiver, and to this day he preferred to take the other road into town, and avoid this part of the neighborhood.

He didn't look away, though. For some reason he couldn't, his gaze inexorably drawn to that hideous facade, those dormer windows like eyes, that gaping mouth for a door.

He suddenly realized that he'd stopped, and instead of bicycling away from the house as fast as his chilled legs could carry him, he was actually getting off his bike and approaching the house, as if some dark and mysterious force compelled him.

Thunder made the earth quake, and he snapped out of his strange reverie.

He'd simply had one too many to drink, and wasn't thinking straight right now.

And that's when he saw it: a pale face was staring right back at him from inside the house! A horrible face with eyes black as coal. It was old man Buschmann himself!

But before he could drag his eyes away from the hideous sight, something exploded across his skull. A sudden pain bloomed at the back of his head. And he knew no more.

CHAPTER 1

"*W*ell, you can't have it."

"Yes, I can!"

"Over my dead body!"

"That can be arranged!"

I sat watching the spectacle like a spectator at the US Open.

"Who are you rooting for, Max?" asked Dooley, who was sitting next to me and enjoying the same show.

"I'm not sure," I confessed. "Normally I'd root for Tex, as he often seems to be the voice of reason in this crazy family, but I feel that Gran has a point, too."

"I agree," said Dooley, which wasn't a big surprise. After all, Grandma Muffin is his human, and if only out of a sense of self-preservation cats often take the side of the humans that feed them. Hypocritical, I know, but there you go.

"I need one of those new-fangled smartphones and if you won't buy me one I'm moving out!"

"Fine!" said Tex. "Move out if you want. See if I care!"

The two opponents stood at daggers drawn, both with

their arms crossed in front of their chests, and their noses practically touching.

"I need that phone!" Gran tried again, clearly not as keen on moving out as her threat had promised.

"No, you don't. You have a perfectly functioning smartphone and that'll have to do!"

We were in Marge and Tex's kitchen, where all good fights between Tex and his mother-in-law usually take place.

"My phone is old—I need a new one."

"It's not old—it's practically brand-new!"

"It's five years old! It's an antique!"

"My phone is five years old, and you don't hear me complaining."

"That's because you're an antique yourself."

"Sticks and stones, ma. Sticks and stones."

"You probably got my phone at a frickin' yard sale!"

In actual fact Tex had bought Gran's phone on eBay, but he wasn't going to let an insignificant little detail like that derail a perfectly good fight.

"It's as good as new, and it'll have to do."

"It's an iPhone five! They're already up to ten or eleven!"

"So? If every time Apple comes out with a new iPhone I have to buy you one, I'd be broke!"

He had a point, and Dooley murmured his agreement, as did I. At the rate these smartphone manufacturers kept putting out new models you could spend a fortune, especially as they kept getting more and more expensive. The latest ones cost well over a thousand bucks. A thousand dollars for a silly little gadget! Nuts. It just goes to show that there's no limit to the avarice of your latter-day capitalist when he hits on a guileless public willing to part with its hard-earned cash. Or, in this case, Tex's hard-earned cash.

"Ma, you don't need a new phone," said Marge, also

entering the argument, albeit reluctantly, as nothing good ever came from getting into a fight with her mother.

Grandma Muffin may look like a sweet old granny, with her little white curls and her angelic pink face, but underneath all that loveliness lurks a tough old baby.

"It folds!" Gran now yelled.

Both Tex and Marge stared at her. "It does what now?" asked Tex.

"The new phones! They fold right down the middle. And I want one."

Tex rolled his eyes, and so did Marge. A collective eye roll. Not good.

"You don't need a foldable smartphone, ma," said Marge.

"Yeah, those things are fragile," said Tex. "Plus they cost a fortune."

"I need the bigger screen, so I can watch my shows on my phone."

Gran is an avid consumer of soap operas. I think she watches all of them, if she has the chance. And the ones she can't watch, on account of the fact that she works at Tex's doctor's office as a receptionist, she records on her DVR and watches later in the day.

"You can watch your shows on the TV like a normal person," said Tex.

"I want to watch them live at the office. It's different when you watch them live."

"Someone should tell Gran that none of those shows are live," I said.

Instead, Marge wagged her finger at her mother. "You shouldn't watch shows when you're working, ma."

"Well, I want to, and I will," Gran said stubbornly. "There's never much to do at the office in the afternoon. Besides, Tex's patients bore me, with all their yapping about their irritable bowel syndrome and their hemorrhoids. Who cares about some old idiot's bowels! I don't need that crap in my life. I want my shows and I want to watch them live."

"She's right," said Dooley. "She always misses her favorite shows these days."

"All working people miss their favorite shows," I pointed out. "That's what DVRs are for. Besides, she can watch them online. Most networks put shows online these days."

Frankly the whole argument was starting to get a little tedious, not to mention repetitive, so I decided to leave them to it, and move into the living room, where a couch was waiting that had my name on it. Well, not literally, of course. But it is very comfy.

Dooley felt the same way, for he followed me out, the voices of three adults yelling at each other over a foldable smartphone following us into the living room. We hopped up onto the couch, turned around a couple of times to find ourselves the perfect spot, and finally lay down, neatly folding our tails around our faces, and promptly dozed off.

You're probably wondering why I wasn't over at Odelia's, enjoying my perfectly good nap on my own perfectly good couch. Well, I will tell you why. Odelia and Chase are redecorating, and the house is a total mess right now. Not only that, but there's a weirdly annoying smell of wallpaper glue and paint that pervades the entire house, and it fills me with such a sense of nausea I have trouble finding sleep. So for the time being Dooley and I have both decided to seek refuge at Tex and Marge's. Fights are never pleasant, unless you love their entertainment value, like we do, but the stench of paint fumes is actually a lot worse, and even deleterious for one's general health and well-being.

And I'd just dozed off and had started dreaming about the birds and bees—real birds and bees, mind you—when a loud booming voice practically had me tumbling down from my high perch. I was up and poised in a fight-or-flight position, ready for any contingency, when I saw that the booming voice didn't actually belong to a human presence in the room, but to some loudmouth on the television, which Gran had just switched on and was watching intently, the volume cranked up to maximum capacity.

"Gran! Turn that down!" Tex bellowed from the kitchen.

But Gran decided to play deaf, and sat watching the TV with a mulish expression on her face. Obviously foldable smartphone negotiations hadn't reached a breakthrough.

"Max?" said Dooley.

"Uh-huh?" I said, my heart rate slowly climbing down from its Himalayan heights.

"Isn't that the guy?"

"What guy?" I said, wishing not for the first time that cats were able to put their fingers in their ears, the way humans can.

"The guy on the TV."

I redirected my attention to the television for the first time. Apart from the noise, I hadn't really paid any attention to the particular spectacle that was unfolding there.

The evening news was on, and newscaster Lauren Klep-fisch, a lady we'd met in a recent adventure, was announcing that a person had gone missing, and asking the public to keep an eye out for him. I have to admit I didn't recognize the youth in question. He was liberally pimpled and had a big zit on the tip of his nose. Not the picture of beauty.

"I don't think I've had the pleasure…" I began.

"The lottery guy," said Dooley. "The kid who won the lottery."

I stared at the picture of the youth some more. According to the report his name was Elon Pope, and apart from the pimples he was also red-bearded and a little portly. In fact he looked like a younger, chunkier Ed Sheeran. He was grimacing awkwardly into the camera, a hunted expression in his eyes. It was one of those pictures paparazzi like to snap of unsuspecting celebrities. Paparazzi just love to make celebrities look like fools, and they must have had a field day with Elon Pope. His entire expression screamed deer in the headlights, and I wondered if they'd caught him exiting some local den of inequity or other house of disrepute. And then I recognized him. "Hey, isn't that…"

"One of the youngest kids ever to win the lottery," said Gran, who was following the story with rapt attention, her anger at being denied Tim Cook's latest toy a distant memory.

"That's right," I said. "How much did he win again?"

"Three hundred million and change," said Gran with a wistful look on her face. "You can buy a lot of foldable smart-phones with three hundred million and change," she added, indicating Tim Cook's toy shop was still very much at the forefront of her mind.

According to the report Elon had vanished without a trace. He'd last been seen exiting the Café Baron, the hipster bar on Downey Street, but never made it home.

"Maybe he decided to disappear," Dooley suggested.

"Could be," Gran agreed.

Dooley might be on to something. The kid hadn't expected to win the big pot and had been struggling in the aftermath of his big win. At twenty-one, he'd immediately walked out of his job at the 7-Eleven where he'd made a career as a shelf stacker, and never looked back. But then stories had started to surface about the fancy house he bought, and the fleet of fancy cars he acquired, and the models he'd been dating, and the wild and crazy parties he'd been throwing, where a bunch of strangers he'd never met before but who'd suddenly become his best friends forever had enjoyed his lavish hospitality.

"He probably decided enough was enough," said Gran.

"Or else he ran out of money already, and decided to move to Mexico and start a new life as a shelf stacker over there."

She then resolutely switched the channel to *Jeopardy*, and for the next half hour intently followed the exciting exploits of Alex Trebek as he guided us through another series of tough questions to guess. To Gran's credit, she guessed every last one of them.

But Dooley and I had had enough. Gran's habit of turning the volume up to the max was impeding with our natural predilection for peace and quiet, so we decided to leg it.

We hopped down from the couch and moved upstairs to Gran's room, which was devoid of both noise and humans, curled up at the foot of her bed and were soon fast asleep once more.

Ah, blisssss…

It wasn't long, though, before the world decided to intrude upon our slumber. This time not in the form of Lauren Klepfisch or Alex Trebek, but our fellow cats Harriet and Brutus.

"What are you guys doing in here?" asked Harriet, who looked annoyed by our presence, even though technically she was the one who was intruding.

"We're trying to get some quality Z's," I said pointedly. "What are you doing here?"

"Haven't you heard?" said Brutus. "Odelia has decided to take us all to Vena's again, so we figured we'd hide in the last place she would look."

I gulped, and so did Dooley. Vena Aleman is Hampton Cove's number-one veterinarian, and Odelia always finds some excuse to take us there and have us turned inside out by Vena's gloved hands. More often than not discomfort and pain is involved, not to mention needles and all manner of torture gear. Suffice it to say we don't like Vena, and we don't like this habit of Odelia of dragging us there, even when we're not sick.

"Oh, my God," I said, raising my paws. "Why can't she just leave us alone?!"

"Right?" said Harriet. "All of us are the picture of health, but still she insists on having us checked out over and over and over again. And Vena never finds a thing!"

"Exactly!" I cried, indignation making me sound squeaky. Like a squirrel.

"You have been having trouble chewing lately, though, Max," said Dooley.

"No, I haven't," I said quickly.

"Yeah, you have," said Brutus. "You told me so yourself."

"Yeah, and you keep favoring your left side, because of the pain on the right," said Harriet.

"I'm sure it's nothing," I said, my paws breaking out into a sweat. "It will pass."

I should never have told Dooley, or Harriet, or Brutus! Of course they would go blabbing to Odelia and now she was taking me to Vena's and I was for it! For it!

"You should have that tooth checked out, Max," Dooley said now. "It's not good for you to keep walking around with a bad tooth."

"You guys, I keep telling you, I don't have a bad tooth! It's all good, I'm fine!" They gave me a look of pity that almost hurt as much as my tooth was hurting. "I swear!" I said. "It doesn't hurt. Look!" I chewed down on the comforter. "Do you think I would do this if my tooth hurt? Huh?"

"It's very soft, this comforter," said Harriet skeptically. "Try biting down on this."

She pointed to Gran's wooden footboard. I flinched, then decided to accept the challenge, and bit down on the board, which was about half an inch of laminated chipboard. Immediately I regretted my initiative, as a sharp pain shot through my jaw, then blossomed into my head like a full-blown headache. Ouch! I let go of the board and had to grit my teeth to keep from uttering a yelp. Of course by gritting my teeth I only made matters worse, and when the faces of my friends contorted in a vicarious pain response, I cried, "Okay, so my tooth hurts a little bit! But so what? It will heal, right?"

"Wrong," said Harriet, who was quickly becoming the voice of unreason. "Teeth don't heal by themselves, Max. They should be looked at by a professional."

"Like Vena," said Dooley helpfully.

"So you're going to the vet, buddy," said Brutus. "Whether you like it or not."

"In fact we're all going," said Harriet, patting my back.

"To give you the emotional support you need," Dooley added.

I shook off Harriet's paw. "I'm not going and that's my final word," I said. "In fact if I never set foot in Vena's office ever again it will be too soon!"

CHAPTER 2

*V*ena was making a face, which told me things with my tooth weren't as good as I'd imagined.

"This isn't good," she said, as if she'd read my mind. Then made a tsk-tsking sound.

"Oh, poor Maxie," said Odelia. She still had a few splashes of paint on her face, and wallpaper glue in her hair. Also with us at the doctor's office were, as promised, Dooley, Harriet and Brutus. For moral support, though judging from their faces and the rapt attention they now paid to the procedure, they were more there as rubberneckers and disaster tourists. You know. The kind of cats that enjoy train wrecks and car crashes.

"Is it bad?" I finally asked around Vena's gloved fingers as they probed my gums and caused me no small degree of discomfort and pain.

"Oh, how sweet," said Vena, who could only hear my meows.

Odelia, on the other hand, understands what cats are saying, and she translated my thoughts to the medical woman. "Is it bad, Vena?" she asked.

"You better believe it, baby," said the large woman. Vena is cut from the same mold that produced the likes of John Cena and Arnold Schwarzenegger and could probably have been a pro wrestler if she hadn't decided to become a professional pet torturer instead. She was shaking her head in abject dismay. "He must have been in a lot of pain for a long time. Three teeth are beyond salvage. Broken off, protruding roots, infected gum, pus dripping from an abscess. Here. I'll show you," she said, and probed my painful gum with obvious delight. "See? And here. See how swollen his gums are?"

I had half a mind to bite down on her fingers, but decided not to. Not out of the goodness of my own heart, mind you, but because I didn't want to risk hurting my teeth even more. Vena was right. I had been suffering quite a bit of pain lately, but had simply favored the other side of my mouth until the pain went away all by itself. Unfortunately it looked as if Harriet might be right after all: toothaches don't simply go away, the way other aches and pains often do. They need a professional's touch to get better.

"So is she going to fix my teeth now?" I asked, speaking a little unclearly as one does when a veterinarian has her fingers jammed practically down one's throat.

"You're going to have to leave him with me," said Vena, finally dragging her eyes away from the devastated area that apparently was my mouth.

"What?" I said, aghast.

"I need to pull all these," she said, as she raked her finger along my painful teeth, in the process drawing a whimper from yours truly. "And to do that I need to sedate him, of course, and then when he wakes up I'd like to make sure he's fine before I send him home."

"But I don't want to stay here!" I said.

"It's necessary," Vena said, as if she could actually understand my heartfelt lament.

"Of course," said Odelia, immediately caving like a true wimp!

"I'm also going to draw some blood," said Vena, and proceeded to bring out a huge lawnmower!

Well, not a lawnmower, maybe, but one of those contraptions Chase likes to use in the morning to remove the stubble from his chin and cheeks.

And before I knew what was happening, she'd planted the contraption against my arm and was using it to remove my precious fur!

"Oh, my God!" Brutus cried, holding his paws up to his head in consternation.

"I can't watch this," said Harriet, turning away from the horrid procedure.

"Does it hurt, Max?" asked Dooley, the third one in the peanut gallery to make a comment.

"No, it doesn't hurt, but it's not much fun either!" I said. "Any more stupid questions?"

They all winced as they watched how Vena, with practiced ease, removed a large swath of perfectly fine fur from my arm, then plucked away the remainder and threw the whole lot into the garbage!

"Hey, I need that fur!" I said, aghast. "That's my fur! You can't just go and—"

"Just a tiny little prick," said Vena, and suddenly jabbed a needle into my arm!

"Owowow!" I cried. That wasn't a tiny prick, you liar!

"Normally I sedate them at this point," said Vena, "but since Max is always such a good boy…" She casually extracted about a pint of blood, then attached a second tube!

"Is that… blood?" asked Harriet, and promptly passed out.

"Oops," said Vena. "Yeah, this is not very pleasant, is it, Maxie, darling?"

"No, it's not!" I cried as I stared at my blood draining away into the tube.

"Harriet!" Brutus squealed. "Harriet! Say something! Doc! Harriet dropped dead! My snuggle bug just dropped dead on me! She's dead, I'm telling you. Dooooooc!"

"Harriet?" said Odelia as she rubbed Harriet's back. "Are you all right, sweetie?"

In response, Harriet merely muttered something about blood.

Vena adroitly extracted the second tube, removed the needle from my arm, then checked Harriet. She smiled. "She'll be fine. Maybe you shouldn't have brought them, Odelia. Cats are sensitive creatures, and it looks a great deal worse than it feels."

"No, it doesn't!" I said. "In fact it feels a great deal worse than it looks!"

"Since they don't know what's happening, and don't understand, all they see is me poking their friend with a needle, so they must all be pretty upset right now."

"I'm not upset," said Dooley. "I just wonder where all that red stuff is coming from?"

"That's blood, Dooley," I said tersely. "My blood!"

"Oh," said Dooley, frowning. "You mean, Vena is a vampire?"

"Just give her a minute," said Vena, placing Harriet on a chair. "Now let's continue, shall we?" She had spilled a drop of blood on her metal operation table, and now pressed some sort of contraption against it. "Let's check his blood sugar level..." she murmured. She keenly eyed the device and nodded. "Looks good. He doesn't have diabetes."

"Diabetes!" I said.

"Now let's have a listen to his heart..." And she pressed some cold thingamabob into my chest! "Mh..." she said, listening intently at the other end of the weird-looking device, and proceeding to poke me all over my tender corpus! Finally she smiled. "No. No problems there. His heart is fine. Now let's put him on the scale."

And before I knew what was happening, she'd carried me over to a corner of her consulting room, and placed me on a big metal plate and held me in place with her gloved hand. I have to confess I wasn't giving her friendly glances. But she paid me no mind.

"Mh," she said after a moment. "He's still a little heavier than I like to see."

"I'm not heavy!" I said, indignant.

"How much do you feed him?"

"Well…" said Odelia, thinking.

Basically she feeds me however much I like to eat. As she should!

"Does he get a lot of exercise?"

"He does move around a lot," Odelia confirmed.

"Where am I?" asked Harriet, emerging from her malaise. "Blood!" she cried when she saw me, and immediately became woozy again. Only this time, at least, she didn't pass out on us.

"I would like him to lose at least three pounds," said Vena now, the spoilsport. "We don't want him to get diabetes, or heart disease."

"And I would like to state, for the record, that I feel perfectly fine," I said.

"You should limit his portions," said Vena, "and perhaps switch back over to the diet kibble. That seems to have done the trick last time."

"He doesn't like the diet kibble, though," said Odelia, and I gave her two paws up for coming to my defense!

"Yeah, well, that can't be helped, I'm afraid," said Vena with a truly wicked smile. "I'm going to run some more tests right now, and then later tonight I'll do the procedure."

"Thanks, Vena," said Odelia, then turned to me, still sitting on that sneaky scale. "See you later, sweetie," she said, grabbing my cheeks between her hands and pushing them together, like humans tend to do with babies and toddlers.

"Do I really have to stay here, Odelia?" I asked with a groan.

"Oh, yes, you do," she said. "You need to have this operation, Max. But I promise, you'll feel so much better afterward. No more pain. And you'll be able to chew again."

"Diet kibble," I muttered darkly.

"He won't be able to eat kibble for three weeks, though," said Vena now. "Only soft food for a while." And she proceeded to pick me up, and inject something into my back.

"Ouch!" I cried. "When is this torture ever going to stop?!"

"Just some antibiotics," she explained. "Against the infection."

What did I tell you? A visit to Vena is like a visit to a torture chamber, or the place where that guy from *Saw* lives. Needles, needles, more needles and diet kibble!

And to add insult to injury, Harriet, Brutus and Dooley filed out of the room, giving me waves with their paws, and then Odelia closed the door and it was just me and Vena...

CHAPTER 3

"*I* don't like this, you guys," said Dooley, shaking his head. No, he didn't like this at all.

Odelia was driving them back to the house, all three cats ensconced on the backseat. The mood wasn't festive, to say the least.

"Never leave a cat behind," he continued. "Isn't that what being a cat is all about? And here we are, leaving our best friend in the hands of the enemy."

"Vena isn't exactly the enemy," said Harriet. "Well, maybe a little." She still looked a little white around the nostrils. Then again, Harriet is a white Persian, so she always looks white around the nostrils.

"Did you see how Vena was poking needles into Max as if he was a pincushion?" said Brutus, who looked as if he'd enjoyed the show.

"Brutus!" said Dooley. "How can you say such a thing? That's our friend you're talking about. Our best friend and housemate."

"Oh, I know, I know," Brutus said without a hint of contrition. "But you have to admit it was quite the spectacle."

He grinned. "Max looked so mad I thought for a moment he was actually going to bite Vena."

"Max would never do such a thing," said Dooley. "Max is a gentlecat, and he would never bite a human unless they deserved it."

"Looked to me like Vena deserved it plenty," said Brutus.

"Let's not forget that everything Vena does, she does for a good reason," said Harriet. "All she wants to do is make Max better. And he did have a lot of pain in his tooth."

"Teeth," said Brutus. "Is she really going to pull three teeth? Ouch!"

Ouch, indeed, Dooley thought. He felt for his friend. Not only was Max going to be forced to spend the night at Vena's —the last place in the world he would voluntarily have chosen to be—but he was going to suffer the indignation of having no less than three teeth pulled.

And as they sat there, Odelia's car wending its way home, it suddenly occurred to him that maybe one day they would be driving home like this, and Max wouldn't be with them, as he wasn't with them now, and in fact he wouldn't be joining them ever again.

The thought actually saddened him to a great degree.

So he made the jump from the backseat to the passenger seat, which was conveniently empty. "Odelia?" he asked.

"Yes, Dooley?" said Odelia, while she kept a close eye on the road.

"Is Max going to be okay?"

"You heard Vena, honey. Max is going to be perfectly fine. Once those bad teeth are gone, he's going to be right as rain, and he won't be in so much pain anymore."

Dooley thought about this for a moment, then swallowed away a lump of uneasiness. Thinking hard always made him uneasy. "Odelia?"

"Mh?"

"What if Max doesn't come back?"

"What do you mean?"

"What if something happens and Max… dies?"

Odelia gave him a quick sideways glance. "Oh, honey. It's so sweet of you to worry about your friend. But I can promise you that he'll be fine. Vena is an excellent vet. The best. She won't let anything happen to your best friend."

He nodded, but was still not fully convinced. Being without his friend was almost like being without a body part, but he found it very hard to put those feelings into words. So he simply stared out the window, while Harriet and Brutus talked in the backseat, and Odelia directed the car to the homestead.

He couldn't quite place his finger on it, but for some reason he felt a twinge of worry. And no matter what Odelia said about Vena's skills, that twinge of worry wouldn't go away.

§

*N*ot that far from where Dooley sat worrying about his friend Max, Albert Balk was thinking dark thoughts about his wife Lenora. She'd sent him out on a fool's errand. She'd told him to go and fetch her the latest *Cosmopolitan*, but when he arrived at the newsagent they'd assured him the next *Cosmo* didn't come out for another couple of days. Darn it, he thought. It wasn't as if he had all the time in the world. Then again, maybe she was planning a surprise? His birthday was coming up soon, so…

He perked up considerably at the thought of finding all of his friends and family yelling 'Surprise!' the moment he walked through the door. Ha ha. He loved surprises.

He parked the car in the drive and got out. Hurrying up to the door, key in hand, he had a spring in his step. And when he entered the house he was smiling in anticipation. No one jumped out at him, though. They were probably in the living room. Ha ha. Funny!

"Lenora?" he said as he carefully poked his head through the door. "Honey?"

And that's when he got the shock of a lifetime. Lenora was on the couch, but she wasn't alone. She wasn't even dressed, and neither was the hunky male lying on top of her. He pushed his glasses further up his nose, just in case he was seeing things.

"Lenora?" he said, his voice suddenly weak and his knees wobbly.

Lenora had the decency to look appalled by this sudden intrusion into her extramarital activities. "Bertie—I didn't expect you back so soon."

"They didn't have the new *Cosmo*," he muttered.

Lenora produced a feeble smile. "Um… this is Hank," she said, introducing the man with whom she was closely entangled. "Hank, meet Bertie, my husband. Hank is a traveling salesman for Berghoff," she told Bertie, as if passing on an interesting little tidbit of information. "You should see the quality of his pots and pans. Really remarkable."

"Oh?" said Bertie, staring at Hank, who gave him an uncertain grin, then held out his hand. It was a firm hand, with a lot of dark hair on the back. The same color of his hairy chest. His head, though, was fully bald, which obviously didn't seem to bother Lenora.

"Nice to meet you, buddy," said Hank the traveling Berghoff salesman.

For a moment, silence ensued, then Bertie shook the man's hand, dropped it, and walked out of his own house, back to his car, and moments later was cruising down the road, in search of a place to stay. He had the impression his life had just turned to crap.

✿

*W*hen Odelia finally arrived home, she let the three cats out of her pickup, then slammed the door, still lost in thought. Like Dooley, she wasn't happy about leaving Max in Vena's care. Not that she doubted the vet's qualifications, or that she would take excellent care of Max. But she had a bad feeling about leaving her cat behind, and would have preferred to stay with him throughout the procedure. The thought of Max waking up in the middle of the night in a cage gave her a sick feeling, and she wondered if she shouldn't ask Vena if she could pick up Max as soon as the operation was behind him.

She entered the house, three cats scooting between her legs, and her heart sank as she watched the devastation. She and Chase had decided to give the house a thorough remodeling. Now that Chase had officially moved in with her, they needed to make some changes. Chase needed shelf space and closet space, and wanted to turn the guest room into an office so they could both work from home if they wanted to. Until now she'd simply plunked her laptop on the kitchen counter but a regular office was a great idea.

They'd also decided to put a stationary bike in there, and use the room as a home gym as well. And while they were at it they'd decided to put up some nice new wallpaper and give the ceilings a fresh coat of paint, too. All in all, it would be great when it was done, but right now it looked like a tornado had hit the house and decided to linger.

Chase was home already, and greeted her with a smile and a kiss. "Hey, babe. So how did it go with Max?"

"Not so good," she said as she dropped her purse on a chair. "He needs to have an operation. Vena is going to pull three teeth. And he needs to stay there overnight."

"Oh, heck," he said. "That's tough. How did he take it?"

"Um… I'm not sure. We didn't have a lot of time to say goodbye. He wasn't happy."

"Yeah, I can imagine. And how are you?"

"Oh, I'll be fine," she said with a wave of the hand. "I was thinking…" She hesitated as she slung her arms around her boyfriend's neck.

"Were you thinking? That's interesting," he said with a grin.

"I was thinking about picking up Max after the operation. There's no need for him to stay there, is there? Locked up in a small cage, feeling woozy, waking up all alone…"

"He's not alone. Vena is there, remember? And the other pets."

"Yeah, but still."

"Let's ask Vena. She probably knows best."

"Yeah, she probably does," she relented, then sniffed the air. "Something smells good in here, and it's not paint or bleach or wallpaper glue."

He grinned, more widely this time. "I decided to surprise you with a nice home-cooked meal. To celebrate the end of phase one of our home renovation project."

She closed her eyes with relish. "Oh, thank you thank you thank you. I'm starving."

She hadn't realized it before, but she really was starving. They'd painted the guest bedroom ceiling that afternoon, then she'd brought the cats to the vet, and she now realized she hadn't eaten anything since breakfast.

Moments later she hopped up onto the high kitchen stool and enjoyed the sight of her boyfriend placing a plate in front of her. It was spaghetti bolognese, the special sauce probably her mother's, microwaved from the freezer. She didn't care, though. She was grateful Chase had put in the work, and she appreciated the gesture.

In a corner of the kitchen the television was softly playing, and she now focused on the image of a familiar figure.

"Isn't that the lottery guy?" asked Chase, pointing to the screen with his fork.

"Yeah. Looks like he went missing."

"Weird," said Chase, twirling spaghetti around the tines of his fork like an expert.

"Why?"

"Missing person in Hampton Cove? And your uncle didn't think to tell me?"

"He's keeping his promise, Chase. He told you to enjoy your vacation, and that he wouldn't trouble you with work, and that's exactly what he's doing. As promised."

"Still. It would be nice to be kept in the loop."

"Enjoy being out of the loop for a change." But she understood where he was coming from. She hated to be out of the loop, too, and wondered why her boss, Dan Goory, hadn't told her about the missing Elon Pope.

But then she decided to put the whole thing out of her mind. She was home, she was with Chase, and other people were probably out there, scouring the countryside for the missing kid. So she dug in, and ate with relish.

CHAPTER 4

*N*icky and Jay were kicking the ball around in the backyard when suddenly Jay gave it a mighty kick and it flew over the hedge and sailed straight into the neighbor's yard.

"Oh, darn it!" Nicky yelled. "Now look what you did!"

Both boys stared at the forbidding hedge, which was high and impossible to scale. Nicky's mom and dad had planted it when they bought the house, long before Nicky was born, so they wouldn't have to see the neighboring house, which was an eyesore.

"We have to go and get it, Nicky," said Jay. "That was our last ball."

"Yeah, I know, I know," said Nicky without much enthusiasm.

Then an idea occurred to him. His dog Marcia had recently dug a hole underneath the fence, and had managed to sneak through. Mom and Dad had caught the reprobate, though, and had plugged the hole. But wasn't it possible they'd done a sloppy job?

"Come on," he said. "I think I know how to get our ball
back."

They ran to the end of the backyard, then behind the rose
bushes, and Nicky crouched down next to the hole Marcia
had dug. He was right. Dad had done a lousy job. All he'd
done was put a piece of cardboard in front of the hole, and
call it a day.

Both boys shared a look, then Nicky said, with a resolute
frown, "Let's do this, Jay. Let's get our ball back."

Jay didn't look convinced. "It's just an old house, right?"

Nicky gulped. "Yeah, just an old house."

Neither dared to mention that the old house was haunted,
and that no one had been in there for many, many years. Or
that a weird smell drifted from the house when the wind sat
in that direction. A smell of rot and decay and... death.

They carefully removed the piece of cardboard, and
found themselves staring into the next-door yard. It was a
real jungle out there, just as Nicky had expected. The house
had been empty for at least the last twenty years, and the
grass probably hadn't been cut for a decade. At first the real
estate agency had hired a gardener to keep the progress of
nature in check, hoping to sell the house, but when no buyers
had showed an interest they'd given up, and allowed nature
to run its course, which it had—with a vengeance.

"Let's go," said Nicky, and pushed his way through the
hedge. Weeds and grass reached to his chest, and the backyard was full of brambles and nettles, but he had a pretty
good idea where the ball had dropped, and made his way
over with some effort.

"Where is that darn thing?" asked Jay as he stared at a
buzzing bee as big as a marble.

"I can see it!" Nicky called out, but when he looked back,
he saw that Jay was staring at something. He retraced his
steps and joined his buddy. "What's wrong?" he asked.

In response, Jay raised his hand and pointed at something in the middle distance. Nicky, turning to look, gulped when he saw what his friend was pointing at. It was the meanest-looking dog he'd ever seen, its fur mottled, its fangs dripping with saliva, its eyes glowing red. And it was making a low growling sound at the back of its throat.

"He's going to attack, isn't he?" said Jay in a quivering tone.

"No, he's not," said Nicky, though he had a pretty good idea that Jay was right.

Then, suddenly, the dog pushed itself off and lunged for them!

"Run, Jay, run!" Nicky screamed, and took off like a hare.

Both boys raced to the hedge, but even before they could reach it, suddenly a large bearded man blocked their retreat, and before they could stop they'd run straight into him. The man grabbed first Nicky, then Jay, and pressed some piece of cloth against their mouths. Moments later, Nicky suddenly felt mighty weak, and then he passed out.

The last thing he thought was that now they'd never get their ball back…

ﾐﾑ

*U*ncle Alec was not having a good day. First word had reached him that the lottery kid had gone missing overnight, and then frantic parents of some other, younger, kid, had told him that their son had gone missing, too, possibly along with his little buddy.

Great. He'd hoped the week would be quiet, with Chase out of the office, and Odelia, too, but of course it hadn't turned out that way. So he'd dragged his tired ass from his chair, had put on his belt and had walked out of his office.

"I'm going to follow up on that missing kid business,

Dolores," he said as he walked past the police station's trusty front desk officer.

Dolores made a saluting gesture in his direction. "Aye, aye, sir," she said with her usual raspy voice. The smell of cigarettes always hung heavy in the air whenever Dolores was around, and Alec frankly hated it. Not that he begrudged her a smoke, but he was a cigarette addict, too, and it had taken him a lot of effort to stop smoking. Being around other smokers, especially heavy smokers like Dolores, always made him crave a drag.

"And if anyone asks, tell them to take a break from crime," he added.

"Sure, I will tell all the rapists, murderers and other scum of the earth to lay off for now, chief," said Dolores. "Tell them that the long arm of the law is tired and cranky."

"I'm not cranky, Dolores." But he was tired, though.

He hadn't realized before how much he'd come to lean on Chase, and with him gone, and some of the other officers on vacation, too, his workload had suddenly tripled.

"Say, chief!" said Dolores as he put his hand on the door handle.

"Yah?"

"Why don't I simply tell them that crime doesn't pay? Maybe they'll see the light! Maybe they'll even get back on the straight and narrow, huh?"

"Smartass," he grunted, and Dolores's raspy laugh escorted him out the door.

"Chief!"

"Yeah!" he said, turning back.

"You're not thinking about taking the car, are you?"

"Actually I was. Why?"

She got up and pressed out her belly, then patted it, and blew out her cheeks.

"Very funny, Dolores," he growled. "Why don't you just come out and tell me I'm fat, huh?"

"You're fat, chief."

"Yeah, yeah, yeah," he said, and made to leave.

"Hey, chief, just give that pedometer a try, will you? You may be a grumpy old bastard, but that doesn't mean I want to get rid of you just yet! Think about your family! And me!"

He made a throwaway gesture with his hand and walked out. Dolores was right, though. He'd installed a pedometer app on his phone and hadn't actually used it. He took his phone out of his pocket and fired up the app, then stared at it. It seemed pretty straightforward. You had your speed, your distance, your burned calories… He cast a longing glance to his squad car, then raised his eyes heavenward. Oh, what the hell….

So instead of taking his car, he decided to leg it. He was a little heavier around the midsection than he would have liked. And his doctor had told him to lose some weight or else… Or else what? Or else he'd drop dead, like Dolores seemed to think?

How far was it to the August place? Two miles? Three?

A knocking sound behind him had him look up. It was Dolores, tapping the glass and pushing out her belly and blowing up her cheeks again.

Yeah, yeah, yeah. He got the message. Loud and clear!

He gave her a wave, and then he was off. He'd show her what he was made of.

Half an hour later he was huffing and puffing, and sweating like a pig, and as he reached the house where the kid Nicky August and his parents lived, he had to bend over and take a breather. His ticker was beating a rapid drum, and he felt dizzy and faint.

Heck, maybe Dolores was right. Maybe he needed to work out a little more. And go easy on the fatty foods. If a crook tried to steal his wallet now, he wouldn't even be able to give chase! And as he approached the door to the August house, he decided to wait until he was feeling more like a human being. Or at least didn't look as if he was melting.

So he wandered to the house next door instead, and glanced up at the facade. The Buschmann place looked less inhabitable year by year. Soon a heavy wind would come and knock the whole place down. And good riddance, too. Who needed an eyesore like that in their town? Out of curiosity, he walked up to the house, then up the few steps to the front door, and looked in. Place was a mess. Why the town hadn't ordered it to be torn down he didn't know. If he lived next door to a house like this he'd have filed a complaint a long time ago. Place stank, too. Rot and mold, of course. And something else. Something he couldn't put his finger on. He stuck his nose in the air and sniffed. Weird. Almost as if someone in there was smoking. Impossible, of course. Unless…

And he was about to apply his ham-sized fist to the door and give it a good knock, when suddenly the door was yanked open and a big, bearded guy appeared.

He was so surprised that for a moment he was speechless. Then he produced his badge and held it up. "Chief of Police Alec Lip. Have you by any chance seen two kids? They seem to have gone—"

And he would have said more, if an unexpected sharp pain hadn't exploded near the back of his head, and the world suddenly turned dark.

CHAPTER 5

I woke up feeling woozy and slightly nauseous. As if I'd been sniffing from one of Uncle Alec's cigarettes, back when he still used to smoke a lot. The smell of his cigarettes gave me the same feeling I had now, along with a slightly metallic taste in my mouth. I was in a cage, and for a moment I thought some horrible thing had happened that I couldn't quite remember. For a moment I even thought I was at the pound!

But it all came back to me when a familiar figure came into view. It was Vena.

"Awake, little buddy?" she said. "Good. I'm sorry for locking you up in there, but it's for your own safety. You've got plenty of food and water so don't be afraid to eat your fill, though I can understand that you won't want to eat right now."

She took her phone out of her pocket and placed it to her ear.

"Odelia? Vena. You'll be happy to know that Max is awake. Yeah, the operation went just fine. He's three teeth poorer but will be without pain from now on. I also have the

33

results from his blood test here—at least the preliminary ones." She checked a piece of paper, then said, "Everything looks fine. Nothing that jumps out at me." She moved into the next room, still talking to Odelia, and I was gratified to know that I hadn't been donated to the pound. I ran my tongue along my teeth. Everything was pretty smooth down there—much smoother than it used to be—and the knowledge that I was minus three teeth didn't bother me in the slightest. I still had plenty of teeth left.

What did bother me was the cage, though. I don't like cages, and being cooped up in one wasn't a lot of fun. I glanced out through the bars, and thought it looked just like a prison. So I heaved a deep sigh, and placed my head on my paws, and decided to take a nap. I was feeling very weak, and before long I was sound asleep again, dreaming of Odelia's couch, and my favorite scratching post, and of course my buddies back home.

I don't know what woke me. It may have been a sound, or it may have been movement. I opened my eyes and discovered that all was dark around me. Night must have fallen, or else Vena had decided to turn off the light.

"Psst," suddenly a voice sounded nearby. I focused on the source of the sound, and saw that a small rodent was hissing at me.

"Psst! Buddy!" it was saying.

"Oh, hey there, rat," I said.

The rodent drew itself up to its full height, which wasn't much. "I'll have you know I'm not a rat, buster," said the rodent, sounding a little peeved.

"I'm sorry," I said. "So you're a mouse, then?" A giant mouse, though.

"I'm a gerbil!" said the gerbil.

Great. I'd just insulted a gerbil. At least it was locked up in its cage same as I was.

"What are you in here for, buddy?" asked the gerbil.

"They pulled three of his teeth," said a voice next to me. I glanced over, and saw that in the next cage a small dog sat. "Sorry," it said. "I couldn't help overhearing Vena as she was chatting away with your human over the phone."

"No, that's fine," I assured the dog, which looked like a Pekinese.

"I'm having my gall bladder removed," said the gerbil, swelling out its chest as if actually proud of the fact.

"Tough," said the Pekinese.

"So what are *you* in here for?" I asked politely. Even under duress, never forget your manners, my mother always told me.

"Worms," said the Pekinese softly.

"I'm sorry?" I said. "Did you say worms?"

"Uh-huh. Worms." Unlike the gerbil he didn't look particularly proud of his affliction.

"Deworming," said the gerbil knowingly. "Trust me, I know all about it. Once they pulled a worm out of my butt the size of an elephant."

Both the Pekinese and I stared at the gerbil. "The size of an elephant?" I asked.

"A small elephant," the gerbil clarified. "But still an elephant. What a sense of relief, huh, buddy? Huh?"

"I wouldn't know," said the Pekinese. "So far I haven't experienced relief."

"Oh, you will. Trust me. You'll feel light as a feather. In fact I wish Vena would pull another one from my butt. There's something addictive about a good deworming. But I digress. So your teeth, huh? That must have hurt."

"I wouldn't know," I said, yawning. "So far so good, I'd say."

"That's because you're still doped up on pain meds. Wait till they wear off. Mamma mia! Though you can always ask for more. Just hit Vena up for a fresh dose. Whimper a little and look sad and she'll fix you right up. I love Vena. Tough but nice, if you know what I mean."

I clamped my lips shut. I wasn't going to extoll Vena's virtues just yet. First she needed to let me go from this prison I was confined in.

"I don't understand why we have to stay in a cage, though," said the Pekinese, echoing my thoughts exactly.

"It's to make sure we don't get into any trouble," said the gerbil.

"Yeah," I said, "last time I was in here I wasn't in a cage, though."

"She must have installed a new regime," said the gerbil. "There must have been a prison break or some kind of revolt or something, and she must have decided to go all maximum-security penitentiary from now on. My name is Harlan, by the way."

"Max," I said.

"Minna," said the Pekinese.

"You know, if it wasn't for the cage, and the fact that I feel like someone just sat on me and then pulled me limb from limb across a rack, I'd actually be enjoying this little chat we're having," said Harlan, gesturing from himself to me and Minna. "Cozy, I mean."

"Yeah, me too," said Minna. "And if only my owner would hurry up and pick me up, I'd feel a lot better, too."

"It's only one night," said Harlan, who was a regular FAQ on all things Vena.

"So we have to spend the night in this cage?" asked Minna.

"Yep. But don't you worry about a thing. We'll pass the time by shooting the breeze and getting to know each other. I'll start. I was born thirteen months ago in a small town across the Canadian border. You may have heard of it, but then again you may not. Coaticook is the name of this small and picturesque little town. Only nine thousand souls, and oh, about twenty thousand gerbils I guess, and for a long time I had no idea what to be in life, or how to apply my very many talents in a meaningful way…"

Oh, boy, I thought as I shared a look of concern with Minna.

This could very well be a very, very long night.

CHAPTER 6

*B*ertie had parked his car by the side of the road and had been idly wandering around. He needed to have a think. It was one thing to hear these stories about men walking in on their wives and finding them in bed with other men, but it was quite another to actually live through the experience yourself. He distinctly remembered having laughed his head off when Colin Firth walked in on his wife in bed with his best friend in *Love Actually*. Lenora had laughed heartily, too, and then when Colin had moved to Portugal to work on his novel only to find love with his cleaning lady, it had warmed the cockles of his heart, vivid evidence that being betrayed in love wasn't the end of the world. In fact it could very well be the beginning of something new and wonderful—and possibly even better than what you had—provided you moved to Portugal, of course.

He didn't feel like moving to Portugal, though. Besides, he couldn't write a novel if his life depended on it. As an insurance broker writing novels was not in his job description.

And his mood had turned as black as the sky overhead, when he realized he was in unknown territory. He knew

Hampton Cove, of course, but this was a part of town he was unacquainted with. It appeared to be a street dotted with only a couple of houses, the light from the streetlamps falling on patches of wilderness and fallow land in between. Perhaps he could move here? It would be a damn sight easier than Portugal, and he wouldn't even have to learn the language. And maybe he would find love again with a local beauty who wouldn't betray him the moment his back was turned. Of course Lenora had always been way out of his league. He'd known it and she had known it, too. But instead of simply coming out and telling him that she was ready to move on…

He had instinctively stopped in front of a large house that looked run down. Like one of those houses you always see in horror movies. The kind of places that are haunted and where only murder and mayhem await the lonely traveler who dares to enter.

And he'd just shaken his head at so much neglect and cursed the homeowner who had allowed what must have been a gorgeous place to fall into disrepair, when he sensed someone standing right behind him. And he'd turned his head to see if his instinct was correct when a powerful blow hit his head. The ground moved up to him with such speed it socked him in the face, and then he was out for the count. His last thought was that Hank the traveling Berghoff salesman must have followed him here and was going to dismember him and bury him in the woods so Lenora could take the house where she and hunky Hank could now both live happily ever after…

*G*ran was in a lousy mood. First off, she hadn't received the snazzy smartphone she'd been hoping to lay her hands on—that nifty foldable gadget that would allow her to watch her favorite shows wherever and whenever—even waiting at the checkout counter, or helping out her daughter at the library, or at the senior center when bingo night proved particularly tedious. And now her favorite avenue of escape had been blocked off and she had the impression her granddaughter had done it on purpose.

"What do you mean my room is being turned into an office-slash-gym?" she demanded.

She was standing in front of her granddaughter and her granddaughter's equally devious boyfriend, both giving her sheepish looks. Behind them, the bedroom that once had had her name written all over it was now empty with a plastic sheet on the floor and a first coat of paint on the ceiling. They'd even removed her favorite wallpaper—the one she'd bought and paid for herself. Little flowers and harmonicas in a theme of pink and gold leaf. That wallpaper had cost her a pretty penny but considering she considered this room her home away from home, and her private refuge, it had been well worth it.

"Yeah, we just figured with Chase moving in we needed to make a few changes," said Odelia.

"I've always had a home gym," said Chase. "And a home office. It's convenient."

"But you go to the gym!" Gran cried, shaking her fists. "Why do you need a home gym when you have a gym membership?!"

"It's for those moments in between," he said. "When I don't have time to head out, and just want to put in a quick session at home."

"And why do you need an office when you have a perfectly nice office at the police station?!" she added, her sense of aggrievement matching her feeling of bereavement. She'd wanted to show Tex she didn't need his stinkin' house and the stinkin' room and board he kindly offered her in exchange for part of her meager pension and the equally meager paycheck he awarded her. That she could always find refuge at Odelia's. Only now her grandchild had gone and planted a dagger in her back—just like that!

"I like to work on my cases at home from time to time," Chase said lamely.

"What cop works on his damn cases at home?!" she demanded. "Alec never works on his cases at home. He doesn't even work on his cases at the office if he can help it!"

"Well, Chase is a different kind of cop, Gran," said Odelia. "He likes to work from home from time to time, just like me, and when he's home he likes to put in a session on the stationary bike from time to time. Besides, I'll use our new home gym, too."

"And of course you're welcome to use the equipment, Gran," said Chase.

"That's Mrs. Muffin to you, sonny boy!" she said, wagging a finger in the man's face. She threw up her arms. "So what am I supposed to do now? I already told Tex I was moving out!" She gestured to her bags, which she'd placed on the floor.

"Can't you make friends with Dad?" asked Odelia. "I'm sure that whatever the problem is, you'll be able to work it out if only you—"

"Kiss and make up? No way," said Gran with a slashing motion of her arm. "I'm way too easy on that man as it is. Because of me he pays a lot less in taxes, and I'm sure he gets all kinds of other benefits, too. And what do I get in return? Nothing! Nada! Bupkis!"

She wasn't sure what benefits Tex got, but she was sure he got something. Why else would he decide to allow his mother-in-law to live with him if not for the moolah?

"I'm truly sorry, Gran," said Odelia, who didn't look sorry at all. Chase even had the gall to grin as she said it. Obviously he wasn't keen on his future wife's granny to move in with them either.

She lifted her bony shoulders in a shrug. "Well, I guess there's only one thing to do…"

"I'm sure that Tex will be more than happy to welcome you back, Mrs. Muffin," said Chase.

"…I'll move into your room and you two muppets can sleep on the couch."

And with these words she marched into the master bedroom and glanced around. She didn't like the wallpaper, she didn't like the furniture, and she would need to clear out some junk to make space in that ugly-ass closet, but the bed would do nicely indeed.

"Pick up my bags, will you, sonny?" she told Chase, then, when he didn't respond, she glanced over to him and Odelia. "And while you're at it, pick up your jaw from the floor."

So who was laughing now, huh?

❧

"We should probably apologize to Mom," said Marge as she took a seat next to her hubby on the couch. Tex was watching something on the Discovery Channel about the migratory pattern of South-African geese but when she joined him he switched channels to *The Bachelorette*, which he knew she preferred.

"Apologize?" he said as he ladled a big helping of yogurt into his mouth. "I'm not apologizing to your mother. She should apologize to us. Buy her a foldable smartphone, forsooth. Doesn't she know how much those things cost?"

"She knows, but she wants to watch her shows."

"She can watch all the shows she wants on the computer at the office. Not that I approve. She should be working, not watching shows. But okay, fine. I'm willing to make allowances. She's old—and she loves those shows of hers. So let her use the PC."

"It's not the same. That computer is old. I'm not even sure it has internet."

"It does have internet. I had it installed when we fixed up the office last time."

"That was ten years ago, honey. I'd be surprised if you can check your email on that thing. I'm just saying, we should all try to be a little flexible."

He glanced over, an astonished look on his face. "Flexible. The way she is flexible? Are you seriously telling me you're caving in to her demands?"

She placed a soothing hand on her husband's arm. "I'm saying we should try to get along. After all, we live together, and a little give and take is the only way to make this work."

"Well, she doesn't live here any longer," he said as he took his spoon and then started scraping the bottom of the plastic yogurt container. She grabbed the spoon and the yogurt container to stop him from scraping, a habit which frankly drove her bananas.

"What do you mean, she doesn't live here anymore?"

"She doesn't. She told me she's moving out and she had her bags packed and everything."

"But... where did she go?"

"Next door," he said as he put his feet up on the coffee table and leaned back.

"But that's impossible. Didn't you tell her Odelia is turning the guest room into an office and a home gym?"

"I didn't tell her anything. I merely registered mild surprise—out of politeness, mind you, and in deference to the fact that she is the mother of the woman I love—and then offered to carry her bags next door myself. She huffily refused and shuffled off."

Marge shook her head. "Oh, dear." She picked up her

phone and put it to her ear. "Odelia, honey? Is your grandmother over there?"

"Yeah, she is, and guess what?"

She sighed deeply. "She's taking over your room?"

"How did you know?"

"Because I've known your grandmother a lot longer than
you have," she said, directing a critical glance at her husband
of twenty-five years. Tex had the decency to look
embarrassed.

"So what am I supposed to do now? She's already asked
Chase to get rid of the box spring cause it's too hard, and
she's demanding we buy back the old wallpaper that she likes
so much and chuck out the one we bought because she hates
that newfangled crap figuring it's bad for her aura and won't
allow her to get her much-needed beauty sleep!"

"Don't worry, honey. She doesn't actually mean to stay
there indefinitely. Only for a couple of nights, until your
father decides to apologize."

"I'll never apologize," said Tex, stubbornly shaking his
head. "Not in a million years!"

"If you like, you can move into your grandmother's
room," Marge offered.

"A house swap, Mom? Really?"

"I'm sorry, honey."

"And all this over a stupid smartphone?"

"Your grandmother feels very strongly about her little
pleasures."

"Oh, I'll say she does. Maybe we should all pitch in and
buy her the damn thing. At least then I'll get my house back."

"Maybe we *should* all pitch in and buy her the phone." She
cocked a questioning eyebrow at her husband.

"Never!" Tex said. "She has a perfectly good smartphone
and she'll use it until it falls apart. And tell Odelia to tell
Vesta I said that!"

"You know what?" said Marge. "Maybe you and Chase can sleep in our bed."

Tex stared at her. "And where are we going to sleep?"

"I don't know where you're going to sleep, but I'm going to sleep in my mother's bed."

He goggled at her for a moment as he put two and two together, then exploded, "No way!"

She shrugged. "Either you apologize and get your daughter her house back, or you sleep with Mom from now on. Your choice."

A mutinous look came over him, as he burrowed even lower into the couch.

"It's a deal, honey," she said into the phone. "Your father will sleep with Gran in your bed, you and Chase can take our bed, and I'll sleep in your grandmother's bed. And we'll see how things stand in the morning."

Odelia laughed, and said, "They should hire you at the UN, mom, as a peace negotiator. Those dictators wouldn't know what hit them if you got involved."

"I knew I should have gone into politics," she said with a smile, and disconnected. "Better take your earplugs," she told her husband. "You know how Mom snores."

He grumbled something unintelligible under his breath, and she smiled a fine smile. She had a feeling this family feud would be over a lot quicker than the last one.

CHAPTER 7

Gran was feeling on top of the world. She'd put on her hairnet and her flannel nightgown and was getting ready to retire for the night. Her teeth were in a glass on the nightstand and she was reading a novel from her favorite writer Danielle Steel. Odelia's bed was a lot bigger than her own, and the room was an improvement as well. And then suddenly the door swung open and her nemesis appeared.

Tex didn't look happy, and he didn't look very fashionable either, dressed in his pajamas with the little Garfields drawn on them.

"What the hell are you doing here?" asked Gran, not bothering to hide her animosity.

"Marge kicked me out of the house," he said a little gruffly as he sat down on the bed.

Gran watched on with a rising sense of panic.

"And what do you think you're doing, young man?"

"I'm sleeping here apparently," Tex grumbled. "Marge's orders."

"But... she can't do this!" Gran protested. "This isn't right."

"Tell me about it. She feels that since you took Odelia and Chase's room, they should sleep in our bed, while Marge is sleeping in your bed tonight and I'm sleeping here, since this is the only other double bed we have."

"There is still such a thing as the couch, Doctor Poole," said Gran, sternly regarding her son-in-law from across her half-moon reading glasses.

"You're not seriously telling me to sleep on the couch, are you?" said Tex, and there was a pleading note in his voice that Gran had rarely heard there before. "With my back, I won't make it to the morning, and even if I do I won't be able to work tomorrow."

She softened. Tex did have a bad back, and sleeping on the couch would only exacerbate an already painful condition.

"I don't understand why you don't have that back of yours operated on," she said.

Tex swung his legs beneath the covers and lay down. "I've told you before, Vesta. The success rate of procedures performed on people with my exact condition is not good."

"I know, I know," she said. She shook her head. "I'm going to give that wife of yours a piece of my mind in the morning. Who tells her husband to sleep in the same bed as her mother?"

"Marge probably thought we'd be forced to settle our differences this way."

"By forcing you to sleep with the enemy, you mean?"

"Something like that."

For a moment, silence hung like a blanket over the room. Vesta kept on reading about the actress who'd been deserted by her husband, whose second husband had died from a wasting disease, whose three children had drowned when their cruise ship sank off the coast of Norway, and whose third scumbag husband was having an affair with the maid.

Tex cleared his throat. "Listen, Vesta…"

"Mh?" she said without much conviction. She liked her reading of an evening, and she was just getting to the good stuff, where a new man had entered the actress's life who looked like he might be Mr. Right. He'd better be, cause she was down to the last pages.

"About that smartphone…"

"What about it?" she said, noncommittally.

"There must be some way we can make a deal."

Gran smiled. Marge was a clever girl. A couple of nights like this and Tex would be willing to do whatever it took to sleep in his own bed again. "Yes?" she said, without taking her eyes of her book. Potential husband number four was married with kids, but his wife had suddenly decided to go back to college, and to dump her entire family.

"Those things are junk, you know that, right? They break down all the time, and besides, the prices they ask are an outrage. Two thousand bucks for a stupid phone."

"You can afford it," she said curtly. And I deserve it, she would have added if that argument held any sway with Tex. Unfortunately, it didn't. Tex had never been all that fond of his mother-in-law, ever since Vesta had thrown him out on his ear back when he was a floppy-haired teenager adamant on dating her daughter. Since at that time his sole ambition had been to become a street artist like Banksy, she'd told her daughter in no uncertain terms what she thought of her dating a so-called artist.

"The thing I'm trying to tell you is that I'm not going to buy you a foldable smartphone," said Tex, interrupting Vesta's stream of thoughts.

She looked up in surprise. "You're not?"

He shook his head. He was lying, his hands under his

head, staring up at the ceiling where, for some reason, Odelia had hung a pink paper lamp with Hello Kitty images.

Vesta pursed her lips. "Is that your final word?"

"That's my final word," said Tex, who could be as stubborn as his mother-in-law when the mood struck.

She flicked off her bedside lamp. "Fine," she said curtly. "Be that way."

"Fine," said Tex, and turned over, dragging a good portion of comforter along with him.

"Fine," said Gran, and turned over to her other side, clawing back the comforter.

A fierce battle over the comforter ensued, which of course Gran won.

"I'm cold," Tex said.

"You should have thought of that before you decided to deny your one and only mother-in-law the one and only little pleasure she has in this world."

No response.

Finally, and because no one could accuse her of not possessing a heart, Gran muttered, "There's an extra blanket in the closet," and promptly dozed off.

*I*t wasn't long before her loud snores echoed through the room. Next to her, Tex plugged in his earplugs, a dark scowl on his face, got up, dragged an extra blanket from the closet, and returned to a bed that was entirely too small to accommodate both his mother-in-law and himself, and tried to find sleep. When it finally did come, all he could dream about were foldable smartphones that cost a fortune, and that kept breaking down and had to be replaced with an endless stream of new foldable smartphones.

delia, who'd watched the light go out in her room, returned to bed. She was worried. Not only about Max not being home, but about her grandmother and her dad sleeping in the same bed.

"They're not going to kill each other," said Chase, as if reading her mind.

"I'm not so sure about that," said Odelia.

"Oh, but I am," said the cop. "If Vesta kills Tex, there goes her meal ticket, and if Tex kills your grandmother, Marge will kill him."

"I guess you're right," she said as she watched Dooley and Harriet and Brutus trudge into the room and hop up onto the bed.

Chase watched them with an air of annoyance. "Don't you guys usually sleep in our room?"

"Yes, we do," said Dooley. "And since this is now your room, here we are."

"They keep following us wherever we go," said Chase. "Have you noticed?"

"Mh?" said Odelia, lost in thought. She hated to admit it, but she missed Max. Silly, of course, for a grownup to miss a cat, but there it was. "Do you think Max will be all right?"

"Of course," said Chase, who didn't seem to share her concern. "He's a big boy, and he'll be fine. Besides, he's probably happy for this opportunity to see something of the world."

"He's seeing something of a cage, Chase," said Odelia. "Hardly the world."

"It is a novel experience, and cats love novel experiences," he pointed out.

"Yeah, but this is not the kind of experience they usually favor."

"He'll be fine," he repeated, and picked up a copy of *Guns & Ammo* from the nightstand and started leafing through it. When that couldn't satisfy his curiosity, he swapped it for *Field & Stream*, which seemed to hold his attention more successfully.

"I'm not so sure Max is fine," said Harriet, much to Odelia's surprise. Usually she was the one least concerned when it came to the wellbeing of her housemates.

"What makes you say that?" asked Odelia.

"When we left him he seemed… not himself."

"He was being carted off to be operated on," said Brutus. "You wouldn't look like yourself if you were about to be cut open with a scalpel to have three teeth extracted."

Dooley gulped slightly. "I hope she manages to put Max back together again. He's not going to like being cut open like a fish."

Odelia smiled. "Max has been through this before, and besides, Vena is a professional. She would never do anything to hurt Max, or any of you, for that matter."

"Yeah, but he's all alone in there, with who knows what animals to keep him company," said Harriet. "He'll wake up in the middle of the night, locked in a cage in a place that is unfamiliar." She gave Odelia a pleading look. "Can't we go pick him up?"

"I'm afraid not," said Odelia, who didn't want to wake up Vena in the middle of the night just because she was having qualms about Max. "Look, I know this is hard," she said as she sat cross-legged on the bed and addressed her cats, "but it's all for the best. As soon as that operation is done, Max will feel a lot better. In fact he'll be so grateful and happy that the pain is finally gone, that he'll soon forget all about his ordeal."

They didn't seem entirely convinced, but still nodded their reluctant agreement.

Soon, she was under the covers herself, next to Chase, and was reading on her phone. She quickly found herself incapable of focusing on the article Dan had written about the upcoming Fall Ball, though, and as her thoughts kept drifting back to Max in his cage she finally came to a decision, and swung her feet from under the covers again.

"Where are you going, babe?" asked Chase, looking up from a no doubt fascinating exposé on tackle and bait.

"I'm going to get Max," she said, a determined look on her face.

"But I thought you said…"

"I know what I said, and the longer I think about my sweet baby in his cage, the sadder I get. I'm going to call Vena, and ask her if there's any chance we can take Max home right away."

"I'll come with you," said Chase, and threw off the comforter, too.

She gave him a grateful look. "Thanks, Chase."

"No sweat," he said as he got dressed and picked up his phone from the nightstand. "I know how much those cats mean to you, babe."

"You do realize that when you marry into this family you get four cats in the bargain, right?" said Harriet, who looked elated that her pleas had not fallen on deaf ears.

Odelia laughed, and when she translated Harriet's words, Chase was smiling. "I knew what I was getting into when I asked you out on our first date, yes," he said.

"No, you didn't," teased Odelia.

"Well, no, I didn't," he admitted. "But I do now."

"And you don't mind?" asked Brutus.

"What can I say?" said Chase. "I'm starting to appreciate why you like those funny little furballs so much. For one thing, what else has the power to drag you out of bed in the middle of the night to go and wake up a veterinarian on the other side of town?"

Soon they were dressed and on their way out the door. Odelia had managed to get Vena on the phone, and the vet had graciously agreed to release her patient earlier than anticipated. She knew how Odelia felt about her cats, and didn't mind a break in her procedure. And then they were off. And as they drove in the direction of Vena's, they just happened to pass the old Buschmann place. They didn't pay any attention to the dilapidated building. Nor to the cat that was slinking along the road, looking for a bite to eat. If Odelia had paid closer attention, she would have noticed that this cat looked very familiar indeed. For it was Clarice, Hampton Cove's most famous feral cat.

$.

Clarice was looking for her next meal. Not that she was hungry, but cats like her were always looking for their next meal. She'd already cycled through her usual places: the dumpsters and back alleys of the town she called her own, and had eaten her fill at each turn. Now she'd decided that what she really needed was something fresh and raw. She liked cooked meat as much as the next vagabond, but she also liked a bit of fresh and succulent meat from time to time. The kind that's still running around when you swallow it whole. In other words what Clarice wanted was a nice fresh rat, or, if rats were unavailable, a nice fat and juicy mouse.

And she knew just where to find them.

The old Buschmann place had been derelict for years, and derelict houses are a breeding ground for all kinds of vermin. The Buschmann house had long been a favorite and popular hunting ground for the feral cat community of Hampton

Cove, which enjoyed the feast that invariably ensued each time they set paw inside the gloomy old mansion. To others, the place might look like a hellhole, but to them it looked like what it was: the best restaurant in town for the connoisseur that was Clarice.

A cat with bald patches, and a reddish tinge where hair was still attached, her finely honed senses detected movement. She'd just entered the basement, and her hunting instincts were on high alert. This is what she lived for: the hunt and the kill. Soon she'd spotted the juiciest, fattest rat she'd seen for a long time. She was already licking her lips, saliva flowing richly into her mouth, her stomach growling in anticipation. And she was just about to jump her prey when suddenly something jumped her! And before she knew what was happening a noose had tightened itself around her neck and she was being dragged along the floor of the ancient cellar. When she tried to wriggle free, hissing and clawing as she did, a stick touched her skin. Sparks flew, and her whole body trembled and shook, then went limp. She didn't even realize what had happened, and even as she was dumped into a dark room she was out for the count, and probably for the best, too.

CHAPTER 8

I'd been listening to Harlan recount the story of his life for so long now that I thought I could probably write a book about the garrulous gerbil. Unfortunately his life story was so tedious and lacking those crucial elements of surprise and intrigue, that any book written according to the lines he set out would have been a real clunker and sleep producer. I know it produced sleep in myself and the other victim of Harlan's storytelling prowess, for even long before I nodded off, my new friend Minna the Pekinese had fallen asleep, too. It was only when a gentle hand rocked me that I finally woke up again.

"Is it morning already?" I asked, still a little groggy from sleeping, and probably from the medication Vena had administered when she'd given me my umpteenth injection.

When I glanced up, I found myself looking at the most beautiful sight of all: Odelia!

I blinked, then actually rubbed my eyes. "Odelia?" I asked. "Is that really you?"

"Oh, look how happy he is to see you," said Vena, whose face now moved into view right next to Odelia's.

"Yeah, I think I did the right thing," said Odelia.

"You did," Vena agreed. "I don't usually release my patients in the middle of the night, but I know how special Max is."

"He is," said Odelia. "He is truly very special."

She lifted me up out of my cage, and I was so happy I was purring up a storm even as I settled into her arms.

"So how is his tooth?" asked Odelia.

"Teeth," Vena corrected her. "I had to pull three. I also got the bloodwork back, and everything looks normal. His values are all well within the norm." She then handed Odelia a box of medicine. "Five milligrams a day, mixed in with his food, for four days. It's antibiotics and a painkiller."

"What about the stitches?"

"They'll dissolve. No need to have them removed."

Odelia massaged the crown of my head and I pressed my face into the palm of her hand, drawing oohs and aahs from my captive audience.

"Max!" said a voice from the floor, and when I glanced down I saw that Dooley, Harriet and Brutus had also come along.

"Hey, you guys!" I said, feeling over the moon.

"Everything all right, patient?" asked Brutus.

"Yeah, I guess so," I said. "She poked and stabbed and jabbed me with enough needles to make me feel like a pincushion, but I guess it was all for the best."

And the best thing of all: my toothache was finally gone!

"So do you have three fake teeth now, Max?" asked Dooley.

"I don't think so," I said. I hadn't really given it a lot of thought. "Odelia? Do I have to get false teeth?"

"Cats don't wear dentures, do they?" asked Odelia.

Vena laughed. "No, they don't. I don't think they'd feel comfortable with dentures. They'd spit them out as soon as they had the chance. No, he'll just have to learn to live with three teeth less, I'm afraid. But he still has plenty left, so he should be good."

"Give us a big smile, Max," said Harriet.

I gave her the requested big smile.

"Mh," she said. "You don't even notice the difference."

Yep. Cats are vain, just like humans, I'm afraid.

I said my goodbyes to Harlan and Minna, and then we were off. During the car ride home, Brutus, Harriet and Dooley kept asking me about my harrowing experience, and I suddenly felt like the belle of the ball, relishing all the attention being lavished upon me.

Soon we arrived home, and but instead of heading into our own house, we moved into the house of Tex and Marge instead, and as Dooley filled me in on the new state of affairs, I found myself curling up at the foot of Tex and Marge's bed, which had now been occupied by Odelia and Chase. Humans. Hard to keep up with their crazy stunts, right?

But I was sure glad to be home again, even if I'd lost a couple of gnashers in the process. I even got to snuggle up to Odelia. And then, right before I dozed off, she said, "I'm glad you're back, Maxie," and I nodded happily. And then she added, as she closed her eyes, with me tucked into her armpit. "Tomorrow we'll start you on your diet."

Oh, God. And here I'd hoped she would have forgotten all about that!

CHAPTER 9

The next morning life had returned to normal. Hampton Cove woke up, its population going about its business as usual. Marge, for one, had decided to throw a nice dinner that night, now that Max was home again, and decided, as usual, to invite her brother Alec to the feast. She secretly hoped that throughout dinner tensions between her husband and Gran would somehow be resolved, and that the good doctor and his recalcitrant mother-in-law could amicably settle their differences and reach some truce.

In fact she'd hoped that conclusion could have been reached the night before, but even though she'd left her brother numerous messages on his phone, he hadn't returned any of them—or even seen them, for that matter. Usually whenever Gran was acting up, Alec was the one who could sit her down and make her see reason, or work out a compromise that made everybody happy.

Marge didn't give it much thought, though. Alec had probably been watching a game on TV and had left his phone in his jeans pocket. He'd see her messages and call her as soon as he arrived at the police station.

Since the library only opened at eleven on Wednesdays, she still had time to put in some grocery shopping, and today had decided to drop by that local institution: the Duffer Store, that famous butcher shop. Known for its high-quality meat and especially for its sausages, the Duffer Store had been a mainstay in Hampton Cove for decades. Founded by the current owners' grandfather, then passed into the hands of the next generation and after that into the current, it was still doing gangbuster business.

The shop's reputation had spread far and wide over the years, and it now attracted customers from all across the Hamptons, who often came into town with the express purpose of buying one of those famous Duffers: the family's trademark salami. The recipe had been kept a secret for three generations, and the saucisse was so famous it had won culinary prizes from every culinary magazine and institution in existence.

Marge didn't often favor the store, as its prices were as exorbitant as its reputation was wide-spread. But on special occasions like today, and to mellow Vesta's mood and make her more amenable to compromise, she decided to splurge on the Duffer salami.

The delicatessen and butcher shop was packed, as usual, and she took a number from the number dispenser near the door, then glanced at the meat display, where an assortment of the most delicious meats and cold cuts were laid out. The store had been updated numerous times throughout its long history, and now looked modern and light and airy, a delight and an invitation to shop. When it was finally her turn, she ordered three Duffers, and was surprised when the man behind the counter, whom she recognized as Colin Duffer himself, said that regretfully he couldn't fulfill her order.

"No Duffers?" she asked in a small voice. Disappointment made her feel weak-kneed. She still had one Duffer left in the fridge, if she remembered correctly, but with six adults around the dinner table, and four cats, that single Duffer would be gone in a flash.

"I'm afraid not," said Colin's brother Chris, walking in from the back. A skinny man with a funny little tuft of red hair on top of his scalp, Chris was small and diffident, while his brother Colin was large, boisterous and had a big head of frizzy black hair.

"We hope to have a fresh selection of Duffers in two weeks," said Colin.

"But… how can you be out of Duffers?" she asked.

"Yeah, how can the Duffers be out of Duffers?" asked the customer immediately behind Marge. She recognized her as Bambi Wiggins, their mailwoman.

"I'm afraid we are a victim of our popularity," said Chris, spreading his arms in a gesture of apology. "We've been selling so much product lately that we can't keep up."

"You have to understand this is still a mom-and-pop operation," said Colin. "It's just Chris and myself, and not a big conglomerate that produces the salamis in China or the Middle East and then brings them into the country in large containers. No, we do everything ourselves. We cure the meat, produce the salamis, and sell them ourselves, or prepare the shipments. It's a long and dedicated process to produce the famous Duffer."

"You can't rush greatness," Chris agreed. "But, like my brother said, we hope to have a fresh batch of delicious Duffers for sale in two weeks' time. Scout's honor."

More voices had been calling out with questions and critical remarks, all expressing their disappointment that the famous and delicious salamis were not available.

"They've run out," said a voice as Marge left the shop.

"They've run out of Duffers? But I've come all the way

from Newark for a Duffer," said another disappointed customer.

And as Marge walked into the Vickery General Store, hoping to buy some salami there, she thought about her daughter. Wouldn't it be a good idea to write an article about the famous Duffer? The salami that put Hampton Cove on the map. Odelia could even ask to be shown the production line and describe the process that went into producing the famous delicacy. And as she pushed her trolley into the store and headed for the butcher counter, she fired off a WhatsApp message to Odelia.

'New idea for story: the Duffer.'

Then she fired off another message to her brother.

'Hey, sleepyhead. Duffers are off the menu. Any ideas for an alternative?'

Alec wasn't exactly a foodie, but he did have his faves, and Marge enjoyed catering to her family's wishes when it came to cooking their family dinners.

She'd arrived at the butcher meat counter and checked out the salamis on display. Then, on a whim, decided not to buy any. Nothing could compare with the Duffer, so why even try? Instead, she ordered pork chops. She'd just remembered Alec loved glazed pork chops, and so did Tex and Vesta. A nice truce reached over pork chops. Why not?

꙳

*C*hase walked into the police station and the first person he saw, as always, was Dolores. Then again, Dolores was the person everybody saw when they set foot inside the station. Dolores Peltz, a red-haired woman with a fondness for mascara, had been a mainstay of the Hampton Cove Police Department for as long as the town could remember. Rumor had it she'd been born at that desk and had simply never left. Long after the last Hampton Covian had died, Dolores would probably still be there, manning the desk and guiding the citizenry to the right officer or taking down their complaint.

"Hey, Dolores," said Chase as he breezed in.

"Shouldn't you be home?" asked Dolores. "Enjoying your vacation?"

"Yeah, well, we hit a snag," he said.

The snag being Vesta Muffin. Tough to redecorate a house when your girlfriend's grandmother has suddenly decided to move in and throw her weight around. So he'd figured he might as well head into the office and let Odelia and Vesta duke it out.

"You look tired, honey."

"That's probably because I am tired."

He hadn't slept well, and neither had Odelia. First the change of location to a bed he'd never slept in before, and then the midnight trip to Vena's, and afterward he'd had a hard time finding sleep with four cats jostling each other for space at the foot of the bed. They all wanted to sleep at Odelia's feet, but since there was only so much space to go around, his stretch of foot space had become collateral damage in the silent battle, and even though he'd kicked out his feet from time to time, sending one or two cats flying, they'd encroached on his territory again and again until finally he'd given up and stuck his feet out the side. He'd woken up with cold feet as a consequence. And a stiff neck.

It was something he'd learned through long association with Odelia's cats: cats always won out in the end.

"So have you seen Alec?" asked Dolores in that croaky, cigarette-smoked voice of hers. She'd probably been smoking a couple of packs a day since the cradle, judging from her wrinkly face and throaty purr.

Chase, who'd already walked past the desk, retraced his steps. "What do you mean? Is the big guy not in yet?"

"Nah," said Dolores, who'd been filing her nails and now blew on them.

"Didn't he say anything yesterday when he left?"

"Didn't say nothing to me. He just left and said he was going to look into that missing kid case, and that's the last I heard of him. He didn't get back before my shift was over so I figured he'd gone straight home."

Chase nodded. "Thanks."

"You're welcome, hun."

He walked on, and passed his boss's office, poking his head in just to be sure Dolores hadn't missed the chief. It happened. But the office was empty. Huh. Weird. Then again, the chief was probably out and about, checking something or working on a case. He often did that, and even though he usually conferred with his people when he was on a case, often, if the case was too minor to bother his officers, he handled it all by his lonesome. Obviously that was what was going on here. So he moved past the chief's office and then into his own and turned on his computer to start his day.

CHAPTER 10

*I*n spite of the fact that my night hadn't included its usual entertainment—and with entertainment I mean our regular trip to the local park to partake in that age-old ritual of cat choir—I was still feeling like a million bucks. In fact I could hardly believe how great I was feeling, considering the fact that only a day before I'd been stabbed with needles, and jabbed with all manner of surgical instrument, and on top of that had been incarcerated against my will in a jail cell in a dark and dank dungeon.

Well, perhaps the dungeon hadn't been as dark and dank as some of the more dingy dungeons in existence but I'd still been confined to a jail cell for a considerable period of time, until Odelia, like a minor Kim Kardashian, had sprung me from prison prematurely.

I'd slept like a log, probably because the others had all decided to give me preferential treatment and had allowed me to occupy the prime real estate at the foot of Odelia's side of the bed, while they battled it out with Chase for a space at the foot of his portion of the conjugal bed—and I use the word conjugal lightly, as Odelia and Chase are not married, even though they are betrothed.

So it was with a spring in my step—well, a relative spring, as it's hard to put a spring in one's step when one is as big-boned as I happen to be—big bones can be a curse—that I arrived downstairs and padded into the kitchen in search of some delicious kibble.

To my surprise there was no kibble in my bowl, and the bowls of my friends were all devoid of kibble, too. Instead, some gooey sludge occupied my bowl. I took a tentative sniff and decided that it smelled like meat, but not a type of meat I'd ever eaten before.

And as I settled down, staring dumbly at the gray sludge, suddenly a voice overhead announced, "Oh, you found it. How do you like my latest invention, Max?"

I glanced up into the face of Gran, who apparently was the person I had to thank for the peculiar sludge.

"What is it?" I asked.

"Well, pureed meat, of course. What did you think it was?"

I stared back at the glop and took a lick. It tasted quite… tasteless.

"I made it especially for you," said Gran. "Following Odelia's instructions, of course."

"Odelia told you to make this?" I asked, my love and affection for my human suddenly trading a couple of points lower on the Dow Jones Industrial Average Index.

"Yeah," she said. "You're not supposed to eat kibble or anything crunchy for a couple of weeks. It's the teeth, you see," she explained, tapping her own dentures to add a visual image to the word picture she was painting. "You need to let those gums heal, buddy."

"Oh, trust me, I understand," I said, giving my absent

teeth a sad lick. My gums felt weird. Metallic. Probably still healing, like Gran said. "So it's three weeks of this?"

"Afraid so."

"Oh, all right," I said grudgingly. And here I'd thought I'd be spoiled rotten now. Wasn't that what humans did when babies or kids got sick? Spoil them to within an inch of their lives? Apparently Odelia and Gran and Marge hadn't gotten the memo on this.

Harriet, Dooley and Brutus had also joined us in the kitchen and as they parked themselves in front of their respective bowls, they all stared at the sludge, their faces mimicking my own surprise at this sudden reversal of fortune.

"Um, so what's this?" asked Harriet.

"Meat," said Gran. "And you better eat it, missy, cause it's all you're going to get for the next three weeks or so."

Harriet slowly looked up at Gran. "What did you just say?" she asked, looking shocked.

"No kibble," said Gran. "Max can't chew it, because of the teeth thing."

"I just wish you'd all stop referring to my teeth," I said, starting to feel annoyed.

"Max lost his teeth and now we all have to eat this… muck?" Harriet demanded.

"I didn't lose *all* my teeth," I said. "Just three."

"Yes, you do. Max can't chew anything tougher than Jell-O, so no kibble or fish bones or whatever for you guys. Until Max's gums are fully healed. Now tuck in, for this is some prime meat we've gotten you. It's got all the proteins your growing little kitty needs."

Her sales talk did little to convince Harriet to 'tuck in.' On the contrary. "This is an outrage," she said, stomping her paw, even though stomping paws on a stone floor doesn't really have the impact one hopes to achieve.

"Well, it's either this or nothing at all," said Gran, who wasn't budging. Gran doesn't have a budgy personality, I should add. On the contrary. She's very unbudgy, so to speak.

"But it's not fair!" Harriet cried.

"You're doing this to help your friend—so don't give me this fair or not fair crap."

They all turned to me, and I could sense a distinct coldness in their gazes. "Hey, guys," I said, holding up my paws in a gesture of defense. "This wasn't my idea."

"It was Odelia's idea," said Gran. "She said you're like the three musketeers. All for one and one for all, though technically you're four musketeers, but whatever."

"If only you'd taken better care of your teeth, *Porthos*," said Harriet, giving me an icy look, "this would never have happened. So this is all your fault."

"Why are you calling me Porthos? And how am I supposed to take better care of my teeth?"

"Porthos is the fat musketeer," said Brutus. "He's also very jolly," he quickly added when I gasped in shock. "Fat, jolly and cheerful. He's like Santa Claus. But with a sword."

"Oh, my God," I said, shaking my head in dismay. "I've never been so insulted…" That wasn't true, though. I've been insulted a lot in my life. The curse of having big bones.

"You do look a little like Santa, Max," said Dooley now, adding his two cents. "With the red head and the white beard and all."

"It's not a beard," I said haughtily. "It's my neck."

"You should have brushed your teeth, Max," Harriet said, not allowing herself to be distracted by all this Santa talk. "Twice daily, or even three times. Once after breakfast, once after dinner and once before going to bed. Didn't your parents teach you anything?"

"Yeah, didn't your parents teach you about dental

hygiene?" Brutus echoed. "Take better care of your snappers, Max, and we wouldn't have to eat this… junk."

"Hey, I heard that, mister," said Gran. "This isn't junk. It's chicken liver, chicken stomach, chicken hearts, chicken necks and… some other stuff. Cooked and put through the blender."

"Did you really make this yourself?" asked Dooley. "You put in so much work, Gran."

"Oh, well… " said Gran with a throwaway gesture of the hand. "It's a labor of love."

"But you didn't make this yourself, did you?" said Harriet, narrowing her eyes at the old lady.

Gran shrugged. "Who cares who made it? It's good for you—and probably a damn sight better than that kibble. Who knows what they put into that stuff? Rat guts, probably, or pulverized beetles. Now eat up, before I chuck it all down the garbage disposal."

Reluctantly, we all started eating from the cold pureed meat, straight from the fridge. It went down like cardboard. At least it was something, though, and after the ordeal I'd had the previous day I have to confess that I would have eaten pretty much anything.

Not Harriet, though, who, after one swallow, declared, "I'm not eating this crap. I'm sorry, but I'm not. I want my usual gourmet food, or else."

"Or else what?" asked Gran, giving Harriet a distinctly nasty look—not the look a loving human is supposed to give a favorite and beloved pet, I might add.

"Or else I'm going on a hunger strike," said Harriet, tilting up her chin.

"Suit yourself," said Gran, and started collecting the bowls, then chucking their contents into the sink, turned on the garbage disposal, and let it chew up all of our food!

"Hey, you can't do that!" Harriet cried, aghast at the chain of events her words had set in motion.

"Watch me," said Gran, and we did. I hate food going to waste, even food that tastes as if someone has mixed in a splash of Drano, but this was taking waste to another level.

"Gran!" Harriet cried. "We have to eat!"

"I thought you said you were on a hunger strike?"

"You have to feed us!"

"Says who?"

"It's in the Universal Declaration of Feline Rights!"

"There is no Declaration of Feline Rights," said Gran. "And when I look at you bunch of ingrates I think a nice long fast will do you a world of good. Now if there's nothing else, I'm off. Ta-dah." And she hooked her arm into her purse strap and was off!

We stared after her, our jaws on the floor, except for mine, because opening my mouth that far still hurt a little.

"She can't do this, right?" asked Harriet when we'd ascertained that Gran really had left the building.

"I think she just did," I said, staring at the empty spot where my bowl used to be.

"We have to fight her on this," said Harriet. "If I have to go all the way to the Secretary-General of the United Nations, I'm going to fight for my feline rights!"

"Good luck with that," said Brutus, also looking distinctly dismayed at this sudden dearth of foodstuffs at our disposal.

"Just watch me. I'm going to fight until my dying breath!"

"Which may come a lot sooner than you think."

Harriet pointed to the sink. "That's waste. A waste of good food. What is Greta Thunberg going to say about this? Mh? She's going to get mad. Mad at Gran. That's what."

"Uh-huh," said Brutus sadly.

"Is Gran really going to starve us to death?" asked Dooley.

"I'm not sure, Dooley," I said. "But it sure looks that way."

And there was not a thing we or the Secretary-General of the United Nations or Greta Thunberg, whoever she was, could do about it.

CHAPTER 11

"I don't like this, Max," said Dooley, using one of his favorite phrases.

"Yeah, I don't like it either," I said.

"She can't do this!" Harriet cried, starting to sound like a broken record.

"Maybe we should go and see what food Odelia has put out for us," said Brutus, who turned out to be the only practical thinker in our small company today.

"You're absolutely right, Brutus," said Harriet, perking up. "Odelia won't go to these extremes. She would never force us to eat this junk, and then throw it down the drain if we decide it is simply not fit for feline consumption."

She was right. Odelia would never put us through the wringer like that. So we walked out of Marge's kitchen, through the hole in the hedge that divides both backyards, and into the house through the pet flap and straight into the kitchen.

It hit us like a cold shower. The four bowls that greeted us were filled to the brim with… the same grayish-greenish sludge we'd already encountered over at Marge's.

"Yuck," said Harriet, wrinkling up her nose. "That's it. My hunger strike is on. When they see my wasted, weakened body, they'll be sorry. I mean, they could have given us some gourmet soft food, but instead they chose to feed us this tasteless, odorless guck."

We all looked up when sounds of a cat eating with relish reached our antenna-like ears. It was Dooley, who'd hunkered down while Harriet was officially announcing her hunger strike, and was eating his fill from the bowl that carried his name.

"What?" he said when he caught our looks of horror and shock. "I'm hungry."

"But Dooley!" cried Harriet. "We have to stick together. We have to show them that we mean it."

He gave her a sheepish look. "It might not taste like much, or smell like much, or look like much, but it's full of the necessary proteins and vitamins and essential minerals that a growing body needs, so I'm eating it."

A snicker sounded from Brutus, and immediately Harriet turned to him with outrage written all over her features. The snicker was squelched, and Brutus rearranged his features into the appropriate expression of solicitude and quiet resolve to go without food for as long as he could manage, or as long as Harriet told him to.

I, for one, was with Dooley on this. And I had an excuse: I was an outpatient, still recovering from a surgical procedure, so I needed all the proteins, vitamins and essential minerals I could get. But I was also conscious of one salient fact: this was all my fault. If only I'd taken better care of my snappers, this would never have happened. And as the cat carrying sole responsibility, I couldn't very well go against Harriet's orders, so I abstained from tucking in, too, hard as it was when I saw Dooley eat with such relish.

PURRFECT TRAP

"You, Dooley, are a traitor," said Harriet. "You are a strike-breaker and a rat."

"I'm just eating," Dooley pointed out. "How can I be a traitor for eating?"

"Aaargh!" Harriet screamed in response, and stalked off and out of the house.

Brutus gave me an apologetic look. "It's because she hasn't eaten. She always gets cranky when she hasn't taken nourishment."

"You mean she'll only get crankier the longer this hunger strike lasts?" asked Dooley.

"Afraid so," said Brutus, not looking too happy at the prospect of a berserk Harriet.

Then, after exchanging a quick look of understanding, both Brutus and I moved over to our respective bowls, and dug in. Harriet might be willing to forego a square meal or two but I wasn't, even if that made me a traitor, a strike-breaker and a rat.

"You know what we should do?" said Brutus in between two mouthfuls.

"No, what?" I said.

"We should go and visit one of those celebrity cats we met over the course of our investigations. I'm sure they'll be more than happy to fix us up with some prime grub."

"Yeah, what happened to Pussy?" I asked Dooley.

He gave me a mournful look. "Pussy moved to Paris with Gabriel."

Pussy was the cat of famous fashion designer Leonidas Flake. After he died, Pussy was adopted by Leo's boyfriend Gabriel, who loved her as much or even more than Leo.

"Paris?" I asked as I moved the weirdly textured food around my mouth.

"She told me to visit her any time I want, but how can I?"

He was right. Cats, as a rule, don't simply hop on planes and fly off to Paris.

"I'm sorry, Dooley," I said. "I know how much you liked her."

"Yeah, she was a lot of fun to play with," he said. He didn't seem particularly lovesick.

"Fun to play with?" said Brutus. "So you played with her a lot, huh?"

"Oh, yeah. Board games, mostly. She loves Scrabble, and so do I. We played Monopoly once, and she was very good at that. Of course she would be, being one of the richest cats in the world."

Brutus and I shared another look. "So you played… Monopoly?" I asked.

"Yeah, are you sure you didn't play another kind of game?" asked Brutus with a grin.

"Um, oh, that's right, we played some online games, too," said Dooley after some thought. "We played Tetris, of course, and Minecraft, and Battleship. But she kept winning so we dropped it. We were more evenly matched with Scrabble, so that's what we played the most."

"You mean to say you never… um… did anything… more?" asked Brutus with a wink.

"No, I think that's it," said Dooley. "Of course we didn't have that many games at our disposal. And we didn't see each other much, either, only when Gabe came over for a visit."

Brutus shook his head. "Unbelievable. And here I thought you two… Well, it just goes to show that youth is wasted on the young." And with these words, he left the kitchen.

Dooley stared after him, a puzzled look on his face. "What is he talking about, Max?"

"Oh, nothing special," I said. "You know Brutus. He gets these weird ideas." I wasn't keen on explaining to Dooley about the birds and the bees. Again. I'd already explained it to him once, but apparently it hadn't really sunk in yet. Which was fine, of course.

"She was nice, though, right?" he said. "Pussy?"

"Very nice," I agreed.

"If only she could FaceTime we could play some more Scrabble. Online, I mean."

"Yeah, so why doesn't she? FaceTime?"

"It's a little hard," he said. "She would have to use Gabe's phone and I would have to use Odelia's phone and it would be a lot of trouble to set up, so... we decided to cherish the memories of what we had instead. Her words, not mine."

"And what did you have, Dooley?" I asked.

He sighed a happy sigh. "A wonderful friendship with a wonderful friend."

I smiled. "Good for you, little buddy. Good for you."

We both ate some more, then Dooley said, "You know what we should do?"

"What?"

"Talk to Clarice. I'll bet she knows where we can find some tasty nibbles."

I shrugged. "Sure. Why not?"

After eating some more of Gran's weird concoction I was ready to try anything.

So we walked out of the kitchen, out of the house, and set a course for the heart of town, where usually Clarice can be found, scouring the dumpsters of Hampton Cove.

"How is your tooth, Max?" asked Dooley as we were walking along, side by side.

"Much better, thanks."

"You know, you don't really need teeth, Max."

"I don't?"

"Not with this kind of food."

"Right," I said, feeling oddly disheartened.

CHAPTER 12

*A*lec woke up and the first thing he realized was that he had an enormous headache.

"Ouch," he muttered as he brought a hand to his aching head. There was a sizable bump where the pain seemed to originate, and as he bit down on his bottom lip to fight the sudden nausea that accompanied the pain, he gingerly opened his eyes. Had he taken a bad tumble and hit his head? But one look at his surroundings told him a different story: he was in a cell that wasn't much bigger than a prison cell, only the floor was dirty and the walls looked ancient, as did the iron bars that formed the fourth wall of his new home. He took hold of the bars and shook them, but in spite of the fact that they looked old and rusty, they didn't budge. He frowned as he tried to recollect what had happened and how he'd ended up in there—wherever 'there' was.

And then it all came back to him: he'd gone in search of the missing August kid.

And as his eyes adjusted to the relative obscurity of his surroundings, he thought he saw a human form lying on the floor of the cell directly across from him.

"Hey," he said in a hoarse whisper. "Hey, you!"

The form moved, then a head lifted, and two eyes stared back at him. They belonged to a red-haired young man, and suddenly Alec recognized him.

"Hey, aren't you that lottery kid?" he asked.

"Chief Alec?" said the young man. "Is that you?"

"Yeah, I'm Chief Alec."

"Elon Pope," said the guy. "How-how long have you been here?"

"I have no idea, buddy. All I know is that I came looking for some missing kid, and someone hit me over the head with a brick or something and dragged me in here."

"The same thing happened to me," said the guy, sitting up. "I passed the old Buschmann place on my bike the night before last, and suddenly someone hit me over the head and when I came to I was locked up in this weird old dungeon."

"So you think we're still in the Buschmann house?"

"Pretty sure we are. Where else could we be?"

"Did you see who knocked you out?" asked the chief.

"No, I didn't. Did you?"

"Some bearded guy," grumbled the chief. "Big, bearded guy."

"A big guy comes in here to bring us food, but he always wears a mask."

"Us? There's more people down here?"

Elon gestured with his head to the next prison cell, and Alec tried to look over. He didn't see a thing, though.

"Chief?" asked Elon.

"Alec," he said. "Just call me Alec."

"Are you—are the police going to come find us?"

Alec swallowed. That was a tough one. "I'm sure they will," he said. As soon as they figured out he'd gone missing. But how long could that be? A day? Two days? And who knows where they would look for him. At least Nicky

August's parents would go back to the police station and tell Dolores he never showed. And then maybe Dolores would put two and two together and send some officers to come looking. He just hoped that by the time they did, whoever had taken them wouldn't have done anything else to them.

"Why do you think they locked us up in here, Alec?" asked Elon.

"I don't know, son."

Just then, a groaning sound came from the next cell, and when Alec craned his neck, he thought he could see a nicely-clad foot and a pair of Burlington socks.

"Hey," he said. "Hey, you there. Can you hear me?"

"Where am I?" asked the voice.

"Locked up in the basement of the Buschmann house," said Alec. "Or at least that's what I think."

"Who are you?" asked the voice, sounding distraught and annoyed at the same time.

"Alec Lip. Chief Alec Lip. Hampton Cove PD."

"Oh, my God. They got you, too?"

"Yeah, looks like," grumbled the chief, who wasn't proud of being captured that easily. "What's your name, buddy?"

"Albert Balk, but everybody calls me Bertie. My wife cheated on me with a traveling salesman for Berghoff. She sent me to buy the latest *Cosmo* and when I walked into the house, there she was. On the couch, buck-naked, doing the horizontal mambo with Hank."

"Who's Hank?" asked Elon, interested.

"The traveling salesman for Berghoff. My wife assures me the quality is top-notch."

"I have Berghoff. I bought it for my mom when I won the lottery. Your wife is right. They're really top-notch. My mom threw out all her old pots and pans. Only Berghoff from now on, she said. Which is all right by me."

"Uh-huh," said Bertie. "That's great. So who are you?"

"I'm Elon Pope. I'm one of the youngest lottery winners in the country. I won three hundred million dollars and change."

"Nice to meet you, Elon."

"Likewise, Bertie. I'm sorry about your wife."

"So what do you think will happen to us, chief?" asked Bertie.

"I have no idea, Bertie. All I know is that someone will come looking for us."

"When?"

"Soon. With the three of us missing, search parties will be organized, and it won't be long before they arrive at the conclusion that we're right here under their noses."

"And then they'll come busting through the door?" said Elon with youthful enthusiasm.

"You bet," said Alec.

"Unless they knock them out, too," said Bertie, "and lock them down here with the rest of us."

"No way," said Alec. "My people are smarter than that."

"Smarter than you, you mean?" said Bertie, and Alec had to admit he had a point.

"It's probably a serial killer," said Elon.

"What makes you say that?" asked Alec.

"I've seen it in a movie once. A serial killer collected women, and treated them really well, until he killed them. But then one of the women managed to escape, and led the cops to the guy's hideout in the middle of the woods, and the rest of the women were all rescued, too. Except for the ones he had stuffed in his freezer, of course."

"At least they found them," said Bertie. "They may never find us down here."

"Yeah, I sure hope they do before this big bearded guy stuffs us into his freezer."

"Everything will be fine," Alec felt compelled to say. "My

deputy is a great detective, and his girlfriend, my niece, is also a fine sleuth." As are her cats, he wanted to add, but he managed to stop himself before he did. It wouldn't add to their faith in him if he indicated that his own hope of being found rested almost entirely in the paws of a fat red cat with a knack for figuring out clues and hunting down obscure leads. And yet he found himself fervently praying that Max was in fine fettle, and already on the trail.

CHAPTER 13

*D*ooley and I had been scouring all of Clarice's usual haunts but so far we hadn't been able to track her down.

"Odd," I said. "Usually she's either at her favorite dumpsters, or out in the woods."

"I don't feel like going all the way out to the woods, though, Max," said Dooley. "I don't think I have the strength."

"Nonsense," I said. "We just ate a very nutritious and filling meal."

"Still," he said.

And he was right, of course. Even though we had both eaten our fill, I felt a hollow sensation in my stomach. Almost as if I had eaten a generous helping of nothing at all.

"I wonder what they put in that meat," I said as we walked out of the back alley where Clarice can usually be found and returned to Hampton Cove's main thoroughfare.

"I wonder what they put in any meat," said Dooley, becoming philosophical.

We decided to pay a visit to our old friend Kingman, whose owner is also the owner of Vickery's General Store, and who is usually well informed about the goings-on in our small town.

Kingman, a sizable piebald, was holding forth on the sidewalk, a crowd of fans and well-wishers hanging on his every word. And as usual most of those fans were female cats. Kingman is a very popular tomcat, if you hadn't noticed. Not because of his looks, because he isn't all that much to look at, but he has the gift of the gab, and never tires from spinning tall tales and dissing out yarns, often featuring himself in a star turn.

"Hey, Kingman," I said now as we joined his group of groupies. At the sight of us, the hangers-on quickly dispersed. I guess our fatal attraction is no match for Kingman's.

"Hey, guys," he said. "So what's new?"

"Max lost three teeth," said Dooley. "And now he can only eat sludge for three weeks, until his gums are all healed up and he can chew solid food again."

"Is that so?" said Kingman, carefully tucking away this little piece of information for later use. Very soon the story of my dental mishap would be all over town. I just knew it.

"Lost three teeth, huh? And how did that happen?"

"It just happened," I said curtly. "Look, we're looking for Clarice. You haven't seen her around by any chance, have you?"

"Can't say that I have. Last time I saw her was yesterday, when she came walking out of that alley over there. Haven't seen her since, though."

"Probably up in the woods," I said, heaving a sigh of disappointment.

"We're hungry, since Odelia and Marge and Gran only allow us to eat the same sludge they feed Max," said Dooley. "So now we're looking for something nutritious to eat."

"Can't blame you," said Kingman. "If I were forced to eat sludge, I'd be looking for some prime grub myself."

"You don't happen to…" I began, but already Kingman was shaking his head, no.

"No can do, guys. If I were to feed every cat that passes my store, I'd go broke."

"It's not your store, though, is it, Kingman?" I said, a little peeved.

"Technically maybe it isn't, but through the law of attachment it actually is."

"And what law might that be?"

"Well, since I'm attached to Wilbur, and Wilbur is attached to the store that carries his name, logic dictates that his store is also my store. If you see what I mean."

All I saw was a bullshit artist inventing excuses not to share his primo grub with some of his oldest friends in town, but I didn't feel like getting into an argument with the cat, so I simply shrugged off his pathetic and transparent excuses and wished him adieu.

"You weren't very nice to Kingman, Max," Dooley said as we walked on.

"Correction. Kingman wasn't very nice to us," I said.

"I thought he was very nice. And maybe he has a point. If he has to share his meals with every cat that walks down Main Street, he'd be even hungrier than we are."

"It's not the fact that he refuses to share his food with us. It's the way he said it. We're supposed to be Kingman's oldest friends, and when we show up at his doorstep in our hour of need, this is how he chooses to treat us? Not nice, Dooley. Not Christian."

We still had no idea where Clarice could be. And on top of that, my gums were aching again. I remembered now that Vena had given Odelia a little box of medication for me. A painkiller of some kind. She probably should have given me some of that this morning.

"Should cats brush their teeth, Max?" asked Dooley now.

"I don't think so," I said. "At least I've never heard of cats brushing their teeth. Dogs, yes. But then we all know what dogs are like."

Dooley gave me a look that said: no, I don't. Please tell me what dogs are like.

"Well, dogs are obviously not the smartest tools in God's big shed, so when a human decides to brush their teeth, they happily allow them to. By the same token, dogs also allow their humans to give them a bath, and run after a stick or try to eat a rubber duck or a slipper. And that's because dogs are known to have a very low IQ. Whereas cats…"

"Allow their teeth to rot and decay because they're so smart?"

"Um…"

"I wouldn't mind brushing my teeth. But Odelia should probably give me a hand, because I don't know how to do it myself. She could use her electric toothbrush. I think I would like that. Though I don't know about the sound. They make a very weird sound."

"Dogs like electric toothbrushes," I pointed out.

"So maybe dogs aren't so dumb after all?"

"Well…" I said, admitting that Dooley was giving me a lot of food for thought.

"I just hope I don't have to have my teeth pulled, Max. It must be very painful to have your teeth pulled with a sharp knife and a pair of pliers the way Vena likes to do."

I winced. "Good thing I was sedated," I murmured.

"Maybe we should ask Odelia to buy us all electric toothbrushes and brush our teeth every night from now on?" Dooley suggested.

I bridled at the thought of a human sticking a toothbrush

into my mouth. Then again, more sharp knives and pliers wasn't a pleasant prospect either, so instead I said, "Let's ask her. Though between four cats and her own teeth, Odelia will have a lot of work."

"They could divvy up the work. Gran could brush my teeth, Odelia could do yours, Marge Harriet's and Chase or Tex could brush Brutus's teeth. And then we'll never have to go to Vena ever again."

I had to agree he was onto something. If I never had to set foot in Vena's house of horrors ever again, I was a happy cat, even if I had to give up a big chunk of my dignity by having a human brush my teeth for me.

"If we do this, though," I said, "you have to promise me never to tell a soul."

"And why is that?"

"Can you imagine what cats will say? We'll be the laughingstock of the town."

"Because we care about dental hygiene?"

"Because they will laugh at us."

"But why?"

"Because cats don't brush their teeth, okay? We just don't."

"Well, we should," he said stubbornly. "So maybe we'll be pioneers."

I smiled. "Maybe we will."

Frankly I didn't know what the big deal about dental hygiene was either. Nowadays with all the pampering going on, and kitties getting massages, and saunas, and facials, and pedicures and manicures, why not add brushing teeth to the mix? Take Pussy, for instance. She was a bona fide Instagram star, and no one laughed at her. On the contrary, cats admired her, and aspired to live the kind of life she lived. So maybe Dooley was right, and I should put aside my petty prejudices and allow Odelia to brush my teeth.

And I was still thinking about this when suddenly a panel van stopped right next to us and two men jumped out. "I'll take the fat one, you take the midget," a big, bearded man announced. And before we knew what hit us, we'd both been scooped up into some kind of fishing net, and deposited in the back of the van. The doors were slammed shut and then we were off, being taken to a destination unknown.

Though I had a pretty good idea what that destination could be, and so did Dooley, judging from his next words, spoken in visible and audible distress.

"Max, they're taking us to the pound!"

CHAPTER 14

*J*acob Turner, mayor of Hampton Cove, pounded the table with his fist. "Where's my Duffer! I want my slice of Duffer!"

Lewis Ferries, who would be his server today, came running. "I'm so sorry, Mr. Mayor, but we're all out of Duffers, I'm afraid."

"Then get me some from the Duffer Store," said the Mayor, showcasing the keen intelligence your local politician needs.

He was having lunch at Fry Me For An Oyster, conveniently located around the block from Town Hall, and had ordered his usual: a slice of Duffer as an amuse-bouche.

This was his daily routine, and one from which he hadn't varied since beginning his stint as Hampton Cove's mayor.

"I'm afraid they're all out, too, Mr. Mayor," said the server, wringing his hands.

"Get me the manager!" the mayor yelled, never satisfied with dealing with underlings when he could be dealing with the brass.

"Yes, sir, Mr. Mayor, sir," said the server, hurrying away.

The mayor, a sixty-something man of impressive proportions, pulled at his white mustache. It was this mustache that had played an important part in his career. Even as a young man the mustache had lent its hitherto hapless owner prestige and a certain *sérieux*, and when that mustache had suddenly turned from its original mustard color to a distinguished white, as had his hair and sideburns, that prestige had grown with leaps and bounds. One look at the Turner mustache and voters knew that here was a man they could trust. A man in whose hands they could safely place their future. It had been thus when he'd been a lowly bank teller at the First National Bank of Long Island, where people entrusted him with their hard-earned paycheck, and it had been so when he'd gone into politics and had reached the pinnacle of his political career by becoming mayor of his town, twenty-five years ago today. The only thing that hadn't changed in all those years, except the volume of his mustache, was the nature of his favorite salami.

He liked his Duffer and he liked it on a daily basis.

Wallace Banio, the maître d' at Fry Me For An Oyster, had arrived and was clasping his hands in front of his white apron. He was a nervous little man with a nervous little black mustache, and looked even more nervous now. "I'm so sorry, Mr. Mayor," he said.

"Stop saying you're sorry!" said the Mayor. "I want my Duffer and I want it now!"

He'd resumed his habit of pounding the table with his fist, and the sound made the maître d' flinch. Other customers were already turning in their seats and staring in their direction. And a disgruntled mayor could very well be the kiss of death for a five-star establishment like the Fry Me For An Oyster, especially in these troubled times, when competition was relentless and restaurants popped up like a rash all over the place.

"I'll try and wrangle one up for you, Mr. Mayor. Please bear with me. Five minutes."

$\mathcal{H}$e hurried away, already taking his phone out of his pocket. Surely there was a Duffer somewhere he could supply to this most distinguished customer.

"Hello, is this the Duffer Store? Yes, this is Wallace Banio, maître d' of Fry Me For An Oyster. Mayor Turner is one of our patrons today, and he wants a Duffer. Yes, the XXL."

"I'm very sorry, Wallace," said the voice on the other end, after identifying itself as belonging to Colin Duffer himself. "But we're all out of Duffers right now. As soon as the new stock arrives I'll send over a box of the XXL with my personal compliments."

"You don't understand, Colin. If I don't get the Mayor a slice of his favorite salami right this minute, he'll go nuts! The man has been gorging on Duffers every day for the past twenty-five years and he's become superstitious about it. If he misses even a single day he thinks it will be the end of his mayoralty!"

"I'm sorry, Wallace. Like I said, we're all out."

"One Duffer, Colin! Just give me one Duffer. Half a Duffer! A single slice! Please!"

But Colin had disconnected. The maître d' returned to the Mayor's table, with lead in his shoes. "I'm so, so sorry, Mr. Mayor," he said, sweat trickling down his spine, "but they're all out."

"Not even a slice?" asked the Mayor, suddenly losing a lot of his bluster.

"Not even a slice."

"But surely…"

The maître d' shook his head mournfully. "Alas."

"Oh, no," said the Mayor, his fingers reaching for his mustache. "This can't be happening."

"I'm afraid it is."

"I'm not going to get my slice today, am I?"

"I'm afraid not."

"I haven't missed my daily slice in twenty-five years, Wallace, do you realize that?"

"I do realize that, Mr. Mayor."

The mayor stared at the white hair he'd just pulled from his mustache with a horrified expression, then allowed it to fall from his limp fingers and flutter to the nice oak wood floor below. He reached for his mustache and pulled at the next hair. Wallace eyed it with a wealth of feeling. Before him sat a broken man, and they both knew it.

❦

"We need new Duffers, Chris," said Colin the moment he put down the phone. "Even the Mayor is starting to make a fuss."

"You know as well as I do that the meat has to cure," said Chris. "Which takes time."

"How long?" asked Colin, even though he knew the answer as well as his brother did.

"We're still collecting the ingredients, fine-tuning the machines. Two weeks at least."

Colin thought about this for a moment. The meat had to cure, that was the key, and they needed to add their secret ingredients to create the exact mix their grandfather had perfected, the recipe of which had been handed down from generation to generation. That would take another couple of days, and only then could they start creating their uniquely flavored Duffers, which came in three sizes: the M, the X and the XL. And for very special customers, like the Mayor and other dignitaries, they also created the XXL.

"We should probably whip up two batches," he said. "With the kind of demand we're seeing we'll run out as soon as the first batch hits the store."

"Which is great, isn't it? We'll be able to raise our prices again, and pretty soon we'll be making a lot more money by selling a lot less product, which is all to the good."

Chris was right, but still. "You don't know how frustrating it is to send customers away, Chris. You're not in the store day after day, having to see the disappointed look on their faces, or to listen to their daily laments. I had to send a dozen away this morning alone, and I'm sure that half of the ones waiting until we open again will have come for the Duffer." He gestured to the display window, through which they could see a line of two dozen customers already lining up until the shop opened again after the lunch hour.

"Just tell them we're out. And that we'll have fresh stock hitting the store soon." He patted his brother on the back. "This is simply business ABC, Colin. When demand trumps supply, that's when people get rich. So enjoy it, and don't fret so much." When Colin made to say more, he held up his hand. "I'm on it, all right, little brother? I'm on it."

Colin watched his brother stalk off through the kitchen, and shook his head. Chris didn't understand what it felt like for a people pleaser like him to have to disappoint people. He hated it. In fact he hated it so much he had half a mind to close the store until they were fully stocked again with fresh Duffers. But of course he couldn't very well do that. So he walked to the door, turned over the Open sign, and unlocked the door.

The first question the first customer asked, a hopeful smile spreading across her face, was, "Are the new Duffers in?"

CHAPTER 15

"*B*ut I don't want to go to the pound, Max!" Dooley was saying.

"I'm sure this is all a big misunderstanding," I told my friend. "As soon as we arrive at the pound they'll see we're not strays, and they'll call Odelia and get this all sorted out."

"We are chipped," Dooley reminded me.

"I know, Dooley. I was there when we were chipped, remember?"

He nodded anxiously, then glanced at the other collection of cats that were in there with us. They were cats of every possible persuasion: American Shorthair, Maine Coon, Serengeti, Ocicat, Highlander, California Spangled, Munchkin, Ragamuffin... Name one and it was represented in the van. In fact it wasn't too much to say the van was like Noah's ark, if Noah had only been interested in collecting one of every breed of feline.

I recognized a lot of familiar faces. Shanille was there, the director of cat choir, Tom, the butcher's cat, Misty, the electrician's cat, Tigger, the plumber's cat...

"We're all chipped," said Shanille, "and we'll all be released the moment the director of the pound realizes his overzealous workers have made a terrible, humongous mistake."

"And then they'll all be fired," said Tigger. Tigger's human is an alcoholic, which is probably why he's always a little on edge. He was definitely on edge right now.

The van suddenly stopped, and moments later the door was thrown open and yet another cat was thrown in with the rest of us. I recognized her as Shadow, Franklin Beaver's cat.

"The only one missing is Kingman," I said as a joke, but no one was laughing.

"Kingman knows how to take care of himself," said Tom. "He knows how to hide, which is more than can be said for the sorry lot that's locked up in here."

He was right. "We should all have been more vigilant," said Shanille.

"How can we be more vigilant?" asked Buster, a Main Coon who belongs to Fido Siniawski from the barber store. "I was simply walking down the street, minding my own business, like I always do, when these two clowns suddenly grabbed me."

"Yeah, no level of vigilance could have saved us from being captured," Misty agreed.

"I think they're doing a clean sweep," said Missy, the landscaper's tabby. "Making sure they take all the cats off the streets."

"But why would they do that?" Dooley asked.

"Who knows?"

"Probably a political thing," opined Tom. "Politicians are always doing things like that. They take a decision and then the next day they take a completely different decision."

"The pound probably hired a new guy, and they didn't explain to him that most cats in Hampton Cove are chipped and domesticated," said Shanille.

"Except Clarice," Misty pointed out. "By all rights Clarice should be in here with us. And the fact that she isn't, just goes to show you this is all one big mistake."

The van stopped jerked to a halt again, and we were all thrown against the van divider that kept us from getting our paws on the crazy driver who kept picking up fresh cats as if we were just so much garbage dumped on the sidewalk for collection day.

The door was flung open again and this time two cats were dumped in our midst.

"Harriet! Brutus!" cried Dooley.

"Max! Dooley!" cried Harriet, then glanced around, and when she met all the other familiar faces, frowned. "Is this a secret cat choir meeting? Did you set this up, Shanille?"

"Of course I didn't set this up!" Shanille cried, indignant. "Do you really think I would hire a human to drag us in from the street and lock us up in this mobile cage?"

"I was just thinking out loud," said Harriet.

"Well, think in silence, because nonsense like that is what kills reputations."

Shanille lapsed into silence, and so did Harriet. Brutus crawled over three other cats to reach Dooley and myself, and asked in an undertone, "What's going on here, boys? Where are they taking us?"

"Consensus seems to be the pound," I said.

"I think they're taking us to be exterminated," said Buster, who could be a gloomy Gus.

"Exterminated!" Dooley cried, and all eyes suddenly fastened on him and Buster.

"Yeah, I got picked up by the guys from the pound once and in my professional opinion this van is not from the pound and the people that took us are not from the pound. In other words, this is not a pound-sanctioned operation," said Buster. He paused for effect. "In other words, this is a private initiative, which can only mean one thing: animal testing and eventual termination. I'm sorry. But that's the only explanation."

I gulped, and so did every other cat in that van. We'd heard stories about pharmaceutical and cosmetics companies picking up strays from the streets to use them for testing purposes, and those stories never ended well. And then there were the stories about a cat-hating exterminator who drove around and collected cats and put them in his oven. Some said he worked for the Mayor, while others claimed he worked for an underground round table of concerned citizens with extreme views on pets as vermin.

I'd always assumed these were tall tales. Urban legends, if you will. But now I wasn't so sure. I had a feeling maybe Buster was right, and that either this exterminator or the animal testing people had decided to wipe out the entire Hampton Cove cat population.

"I've heard stories," Brutus now also intimated. "Stories about cat haters working with a hired gun. They consider cats a menace, and want to get rid of us once and for all. Accuse us of being silent killers of birds and other species, and want to make us extinct."

I'd heard the stories, too, about an island in Australia where thousands of cats were marked for termination, with traps and toxins. Or towns where a cat curfew is in effect, and owners are advised to keep their cats indoors from sundown to sunup. Or else…

I gulped some more, hoping Buster was wrong, and so was Brutus. Because if they were right… this just might be the end. And I wasn't feeling entirely fit to fight our opponent right then, what with having recently suffered the indignant loss of three teeth. If only I still had those teeth, I could have bit my way out of this predicament.

Oh, damn you, Vena. Damn you and your pliers!

CHAPTER 16

*D*olores had been fielding calls all afternoon, mainly from cat owners who were calling in to announce that their precious little fur babies had gone missing. She'd been carefully writing everything down, and had been sending word to the officers to take these cases in hand. Unfortunately there wasn't a lot of enthusiasm to find these cats, with most officers clearly feeling cats could take care of themselves. But when the parents of Nicky August called again, asking why the chief had never shown up, she got up from her perch and marched over to Chase's office and entered without knocking.

"Chase, the parents of that missing munchkin just called again. The chief never showed up to take their statement, and now they're wondering if they should talk to the media, cause they're pretty much on the verge of giving up on the police altogether."

"Yeah, I know," said Chase, looking distraught. "I've been trying the chief's cell all morning, and he doesn't pick up."

"That's not like him," said Dolores, who'd known the chief

from when he was a beat cop, and had seen his slow rise through the ranks to the position he held now.

"No, that's absolutely not like him at all. Where was he going when he left here?"

"I told you already, to talk to the parents of the missing kid—Nicky August."

"Better call them back and tell them I'm on my way," said Chase as he got up from behind his desk.

"You're going to handle this yourself? I can always send one of the uniforms."

"No, they deserve an official apology, and maybe I can figure out what happened to the chief."

"Oh, and a bunch of people are calling about their missing cats," said Dolores.

"Missing cats?"

"At least a dozen reports so far. I've handed them to your colleagues, but they're less than excited at the prospect of looking for a bunch of missing pets." They both looked in at the office, which was open-plan, with desks dotting the cluttered space. None of the other officers appeared particularly busy, and Chase heaved a disappointed sigh.

"When the cat's away…" said Dolores with a shrug.

Chase clapped his hands. "Listen up!" he said. Instantly, they all sat up with a jerk. "Let's get on this missing cats business, all right? They may only be pets, but that doesn't mean they're not important. So divide up the work and let's get cracking, people!"

❧

*A*t the office, Odelia was adding some spice to the article Dan had written about the upcoming Fall Ball, always a big thing in Hampton Cove, and an opportunity for the mayor to mingle with his constituents. The next election was still three years away, but Mayor Turner never missed an opportunity to sell himself to potential voters. Maybe the reason he'd been in office for as long as Odelia could remember. Suddenly Dan stuck his head in the door.

"Have you heard about the case of the missing Duffer?" he asked with a slight grin on his bearded face.

"The missing what?" she asked, looking up from her laptop.

"The missing Duffer. The famous salami?"

She leaned back. "Funny. My mom sent me a text this morning about the Duffer. How does a sausage go missing, exactly?" This sounded like a story right up Dan's alley. He liked to fill the *Gazette* with colorful fluff pieces like that. And readers loved it.

"Take the story and find out. The Mayor made a big scene at Fry Me For An Oyster when they announced they were all out of Duffers. Threatened to fire the entire staff."

"He can't fire the staff. He doesn't own the restaurant. Does he?"

"Who knows with these local moguls."

"Is this really a story we need to pursue, Dan?" she asked, gesturing to the pile of files clogging up her inbox.

Dan arched an eyebrow. "The Mayor? Blowing his top? Over a sausage?"

She grinned. "I see your point. But can you finish this article about the Fall Ball?"

"Will do, kid," said Dan, rapping his knuckles on the doorjamb and returning to his own sanctum.

She picked up her bag, which held a dictaphone, laptop, and enough notebooks to write up a dozen stories about a dozen mayors blowing their tops over a lack of salamis.

She walked the short distance to the restaurant where the sordid scene had played out, and ten minutes later she was talking to one of the servers who'd actually witnessed the incident, and gave a vivid blow-by-blow account of the Mayor's darkest moment.

Next came Wallace Banio, the maître d', who was more than happy to spill the beans, provided his name wasn't mentioned in the article. "I don't know what came over him," he said. "He went completely berserk. Said that if I didn't feed him his daily slice of Duffer, he'd ruin me, ruin my family, ruin the restaurant, and see to it that I never worked in this town again. Do you think he can do that, Miss Poole?"

"I doubt it," said Odelia. "You have to remember that politicians live at the mercy of the voting public. They're only one vote away from being replaced by the next guy."

Wallace nodded, visibly relieved. "At the end, he got a little sad, though. He seemed to realize he'd made a big fuss over nothing. I actually felt sorry for the poor guy. He acted like an addict, you know. A Duffer addict."

"So maybe he should join the ADs. The Anonymous Dufferaholics?" The joke didn't register, though, but then Odelia's jokes rarely did. Maybe she wasn't a born comedian.

Next on her list was the source of all the trouble: the Duffer Store, where those precious Duffers were sold.

When she arrived, though, a sign on the door said that the store was closed, which was odd, as it wasn't even three o'clock yet. An old lady who'd arrived at the same time as her, shook her permed purple head. "Bad business, Miss Poole. Bad business."

"Oh, and why is that?"

"I've been buying my Duffers here for years—my husband loves his daily slice of Duffer right before going to bed, and so do I, frankly speaking, and little Fifi, of course."

"Your son?"

"Dog. Oh, does she love her Duffers. And now, for the first time in all these years, they're out of Duffers! Can you imagine? My husband is going nuts. Fifi is going nuts. I had a small stash of Duffers that I kept in the pantry, like all Duffer lovers do, but then the night before last we ate our last slice. I know it was careless of me to leave my shopping to the last minute, and normally I never do, and then wouldn't you know it?"

"No more Duffers?"

"No more Duffers! What is the world coming to, Miss Poole? This is a tragedy."

"Uh-huh," said Odelia. "Sure."

The story was starting to get to her. It was often that way. A good story needed to cure a little. Like a Duffer. It started out small and silly, and then turned into a real whopper. "So where do they live, these Duffers? The people, I mean, not the sausages."

The woman stared at her, appalled. "Never," she said, wagging a reproachful finger, "never call a Duffer a sausage. It's a salami. A *saucisse*. Write that down, will you?"

She dutifully wrote it down. "Saucisse not sausage," she muttered.

"They used to live over the store, but that was a long time ago. Nowadays they live in some big mansion out of town. Along what they call the Billionaire Mile. Of course back in my day it was called the Millionaire Mile, but I guess that's inflation for ya, huh?"

"I guess."

The woman was eyeing her intently. "Do you know that even the President of the United States of America loves his Duffer of a morning?"

"That wouldn't surprise me."

"Well, he does. So there you go." And having delivered this bit of inside information into the world of the Duffer, she pottered off, probably to break the terrible news to her husband and Fifi that the Duffer Store had run out of Duffers.

Odelia's phone chimed, and she fished it out of her bag. It was Dan.

"And? Did you talk to the Mayor?" asked the veteran newspaperman. "I would love to see his face when you confront him with his temper tantrum over a slice of sausage."

"Never call a Duffer a sausage, Dan," she said sternly. "It's a saucisse."

"I can tell this Duffer business is getting to you, honey. Stay objective, all right?"

"I'm just kidding, Dan. But the Duffer clientele clearly isn't. The mayor isn't the only one going nuts over this sudden Duffer dearth."

"Duffer dearth. Nice one."

"Yeah. It's a real Duffer *dry* spell. Get it? Because salamis are air-dried?"

"Yah. Maybe you should stick to being a reporter."

She cleared her throat. "So do you have any idea where I can find these Duffers?"

She heard the sound of keys clacking, then Dan came back with an address.

She whistled. "Nice digs."

"Yeah. I should have gone into the sausage business."

"Saucisse, Dan. Saucisse."

"Yeah, yeah."

She got back into her car and was just about to drive off when her phone jangled again. When she saw it was Chase, she picked up with a cheerful, "Howdy, stranger."

"Howdy," said Chase, sounding a lot less chipper.

"What's wrong?" she asked.

"The weirdest thing. First off, your uncle seems to have gone missing."

"That is weird."

"Yeah, and secondly, all of Hampton Cove's cats have gone missing, too."

"What?"

"We've been getting dozens of calls from worried pet owners. Only cats, though, not dogs or parakeets or whatever, which is kind of specific, don't you think? Not to mention strange."

"Yeah," she said, a worried frown creasing her brow. "Have you called Gran to ask—"

"About your cats? I have, but she's at the office, so she has no idea. And your mom is at the library so she doesn't know either. She promised to call me as soon as she gets home."

"So… about my uncle?" she said slowly, thinking about the missing cats mystery. How strange that all the cats of Hampton Cove would suddenly go missing for some reason.

"Unfortunately he didn't take the car, so I have no idea where he went."

"He walked?"

"I know."

"It's not like my uncle to not take the car to go anywhere."

"He has a pedometer app on his phone, so I guess he decided to use it."

"Mh."

"So what are you up to?"

"Doing a story on the missing Duffer."

"Duffer? I don't remember seeing a report about a missing person called Duffer."

"You wouldn't. The Duffer is a famous saucisse, a local delicacy."

"Ah, that Duffer."

Like practically everyone in Hampton Cove, Chase had fallen for the seductive charm and lingering aroma of the delicious salami. And as Odelia drove out to the Billionaire

Mile, where all the celebs lived on a narrow stretch of exclusive beachfront property, she thought about her cats, and hoped they were fine. Then again, why wouldn't they be? She'd taught them never to talk to strangers—human strangers, not feline ones.

CHAPTER 17

The van had been picking up more and more 'passengers' like a regular bus route, but at the next stop no door was being opened and no fresh prisoners were being dumped in. The van was full to overflowing, and since there was no room left, and we were all packed solid, the atmosphere was frankly becoming a little uncomfortable.

"I have to wee, Max," Dooley whispered into my ear.

"Well, you'll have to hold it up for now," I said. "Unless you want to turn this van into a toilet, and all these other cats into very angry travelers."

"I know," he said, looking as pained as only he can look. "But I really have to go, Max. I've been holding it in for fifteen minutes already and I'm going to burst if I don't go."

"Maybe you can pee through that crack in the floor," said Brutus, indicating a small crack where sunlight peeked in and through which we could see a small patch of asphalt.

"Gee, thanks," said Dooley gratefully, and aimed very precisely indeed, peeing straight through the crack.

Moments later, a growly voice right outside announced,

"Damn oil leaks," and a loud thunk on the side of the van told us the driver had exited and was standing next to us.

Harriet giggled, in spite of the circumstances. "He thinks Dooley's wee is an oil leak."

"Yeah, very funny," I agreed, though I wasn't laughing.

I now noticed for the first time that the engine had been turned off, which told me that we might have reached our destination, wherever it was. The other cats had come to the same conclusion, for they all started to chatter nervously.

"I say we make a run for it the moment those doors are opened," said Tom, who likes to think he's tough but is actually a scaredy-cat.

"And I say we don't do a thing," said Shanille, whose position as cat choir's supreme leader tends to lend her a modicum of authority in our small feline community.

"What are you talking about?" asked Tom. "If we don't take a stand now and fight our way out, who knows where we'll end up?"

"We'll all end up back home where we belong," said Shanille snippily. "This is all some kind of mistake, obviously, and as soon as everything is cleared up we'll be escorted home with a full apology and that will be that."

"An adventure to remember," said Shadow happily, then sniffed the air. "What's that smell?"

All eyes now turned to Dooley, who apparently hadn't aimed as well as he'd anticipated.

"Dooley!" cried Buster. "I know it's you. I'd recognize that scent anywhere!"

And he would. We all would. Cats can easily recognize the scent of another cat, even if we've only met once. In fact it's one of our strong suits, though it was a little annoying now, not to mention embarrassing, and Dooley made himself as small as he could, which is hard when you're in the same cramped space as all of your accusers.

But then suddenly the door was thrown open, and half of the cats seemed to have made up their minds to follow Tom's advice, and stormed towards the exit. They quickly disappeared from view, and then it was just us stragglers.

"Out!" shouted a male voice. "Out right now!" And to make his meaning perfectly clear, he thunked the side of the van with his fist, creating a loud ruckus that frankly was very disagreeable to our highly sensitive ears. So we all got out of the van, and were led down a short sort of ramp and then into what looked like a basement of some kind.

It all smelled very foul, I don't mind telling you. Like rot and damp and mustiness.

"This doesn't look like the pound, Max," said Brutus as we looked around the place.

"No, it doesn't," I agreed. "It looks more like the basement of a very old house."

It was cavernous, too, with an arched brick ceiling, where moss was growing, and the floor was an earthen one, also moss-covered. There was a definite nip in the air that I found particularly unenjoyable. As if someone had left the windows open for a long time.

The cats that had led the charge out of the van, and had hoped to secure their escape, were also there, so their brave attempt had been for naught, a fact that didn't appear to sit well with them, for they were all muttering dark oaths under their breaths.

There only seemed to be one entrance, the one through which we'd been dumped, and as I listened intently I could hear the van now driving off again. It had simply backed up against the only window into the place, and had deposited all of us inside this cellar.

"Looks like some underground prison," said Brutus as we all huddled together.

"Hey there," suddenly spoke a cat we all knew very well.

"Clarice!" I cried. "What are you doing here?" Only now did I notice there were a lot more cats down there than had fit inside that van.

"Actually I came here looking for a nice rat to eat," she said, ambling up to us. "What I found was some nasty human who grabbed me and threw me into this old dungeon."

"So this is what a dungeon looks like," said Dooley, glancing around with interest.

"But Clarice," said Harriet. "If you're here, that means…"

We were all silent as the thought entered our minds that if Clarice was here, *the* Clarice, most vigilant, self-sufficient and toughest cat Hampton Cove had ever known, that things looked very bad indeed.

"How come they took you?" asked Buster. "You're not even chipped."

He expressed one of those old prejudices some domesticated cats have against their feral brethren and sistren. As if being domesticated and chipped makes a cat superior to the non-chipped variety.

"Chipped or not chipped, we're all in the same boat here," said Clarice.

"And what boat would that be?" asked Dooley.

"I have no idea. But judging from that smell there's a dog on the premises."

I stuck my nose in the air and sniffed. Clarice was right. I clearly smelled a dog. And then I heard it: the low, menacing growl of a dog who smells cats. It seemed to be coming from outside, from the small window through which we'd been dumped down here. Yikes!

"I hope this isn't some kind of cult," said Shanille. "I hate cults."

"You mean, like a cat-worshipping cult?" asked Dooley. "I saw a documentary about a cat-worshipping cult on the Discovery Channel once."

"Enough with the Discovery Channel already, Dooley!" cried Harriet.

"No, let him finish," said Clarice. "What did they say?"

"Oh, just that there are cults that worship cats, just like the Egyptians did. The Egyptians liked cats so much that they buried them along with them, to accompany them into the hereafter." He slung a paw in front of his face when the meaning of his words came home to him. "Oh, no. Do you think they're going to bury us with a pharaoh?"

"I don't think they still have pharaohs," said Brutus. "Not that I know of, at least."

"No, pharaohs don't exist anymore," I said. "But maybe a cat-worshipping cult does exist, and they've decided to collect us for some kind of ritual. Which isn't necessarily a bad thing," I quickly added as murmurs of panic spread through the dank and dingy dungeon. "Maybe it's a nice cult, and they just want us around for our positive vibes."

"Or maybe they'll kill us all and bury us in some old creep's coffin," said Clarice.

CHAPTER 18

Odelia parked her car by the side of the road and got out, hiking her bag up her shoulder. She looked up at the towering gate that protected the property of the Duffer family and wondered how many of these mansions she would visit before her surprise at the opulence of some people's residences would diminish. In all the years she'd been a reporter for the *Hampton Cove Gazette* she'd interviewed so many of the super-rich and still she was in awe each time she entered another one of their palaces. And the palace that the Duffers had built promised to be another doozy. She felt a little sorry that Chase wasn't there to accompany her, or her cats. Even Gran would have been welcome, but she was so busy being angry with the rest of the family she'd ceased to offer her unique services. At least until Tex finally caved and decided to buy her a foldable smartphone.

Gran was like a child. Once she had her mind set on some toy she couldn't stop nagging and making everyone's life miserable until she got what she wanted.

But weren't most people like that, though? Kids wanted

Playstations or Barbie dolls and grownups wanted the latest iPhone or a Netflix subscription or some Star Wars collectible. The principle was the same, only the price tag increased exponentially.

She rang the bell, and when a voice asked her to state her name and business she clearly spoke her name into the inter-com, and said she wanted to ask about the recent Duffer dearth. Immediately the gate buzzed open and she pushed through and onto the drive. She wondered for a moment whether to take the car, but she could already see the house just around the corner, hidden from view if you stood in front of the gate. So she marched on and was soon greeted by a homely-looking woman at the door who invited her in and said she'd get Mr. Duffer for her and would she please wait in the sitting room.

The house was smaller than she'd anticipated, and looked more like an old mansion than a modern McMansion. On the outside it was all red brick and ivy, and the windows still had wooden shutters, which had recently been painted a vivid green. The roof and the gutters looked new, too, and once inside she was surprised by how cozy the house was. Exposed brick, modern stone floors and wood beam ceilings were all nicely done.

She took a seat in the sitting room, where a collection of gate-leg tables laden with knickknacks and comfortable linen sofas lent the room a pleasant atmosphere. A big coffee table supported an impressive coffee-table book that claimed to be the definitive guide on all things sausage through the ages. And she'd just started leafing through it when a large man entered the room. He had a black ring beard and a round belly that protruded past his cable-knit cardigan. He was also smoking a pipe, which seemed odd, given that indoor smoking was probably a thing of the past, or so she'd always thought. Then again, since some salamis are supposed to be made from smoked meat...

"I'm sorry," said the man, looking a little distracted, "but, um, who are you again?"

"My name is Poole. Odelia Poole. I'm a reporter with the *Hampton Cove Gazette*, and I was hoping to glean some background information on the Duffer. Your famous salami?" she added when he gave her a curious look.

"Oh, yes, right. Of course. The Duffer. My family's pride and joy. Well, what do you want to know?" he asked, gesturing to the linen sofa with flower motif and taking a seat in an overstuffed chair himself. As he sat down, it creaked under his considerable bulk. "My name is Colin, by the way," he said as he put out his pipe and steepled his fingers. "I hope it's me you wanted and not my brother Chris. We both live here, though occupying separate wings, of course. He's not home right now, or else he would have..." He frowned. "Chris is more the PR person in our family. I'm the one in charge of the Duffer Store." He gave her a pained look. "If only you'd made an appointment... Chris has this whole PR spiel down to a science, you see. And I'm afraid I'm not going to be much help to you."

"Oh, but that's fine," she said. "This story more or less landed in my lap when Mayor Turner had a nervous breakdown when he discovered his restaurant was out of Duffers."

Colin produced a small smile. "Did he now? A nervous breakdown, you say?"

"He threatened to fire the entire staff if they didn't give him his daily Duffer."

"Daily Duffer. I like that. Well, he will soon have his daily Duffer again, I can assure you, Miss Poole. We're merely experiencing some inventory management issues."

"What is it about the Duffer that makes people so crazy about it?" she asked, taking out her notebook and a pen.

He stared at both items for a moment, then said in a modest tone, "Oh, well, I guess you'd have to ask them—our customers, I mean. They're best placed to tell you that."

"No, but what is in it? What makes it so different from every other sausage out there?"

"Have you tasted the Duffer, Miss Poole?"

"Oh, sure. At least I think I have. I'm not a big sausage person myself, actually."

"Oh, so you think you have. Well, let me begin by telling you that if you merely think you have tasted the Duffer you haven't sampled a real Duffer. Once eaten, the Duffer is not an experience one lightly forgets."

"My grandmother likes it, and so does my mom," she said, hoping she hadn't insulted Mr. Duffer with her lack of first-hand Duffer knowledge.

Colin Duffer picked up a small silver bell from the coffee table and jangled it. Instantly the same lady who'd opened the door for her came hurrying in. "Maria, could you please bring us a few slices of the Duffer XXXL?" he said.

"Of course, sir," said Maria, then hurried off again.

"The Duffer's ingredients are not all that different from any other saucisse out there," said Colin. "The word salami originates from *sale*, Italian for salt, which is an important ingredient. Basically salami is salted and spiced meat, dried and fermented. The traditional salami is made from beef or pork, while some contain poultry, mainly turkey. Typical seasonings include garlic, minced fat, white pepper, herbs, vinegar, wine… The fermented mixture isn't cooked but cured and dried. The only difference between other salamis and the Duffer is in the secret ingredient that my grandfather discovered and which adds to the very particular flavor which, once tasted, you'll never forget."

"Secret ingredient, huh? Like Coca Cola, you mean?"

He smiled indulgently. "Yes. Like Coca Cola, my family

uses a secret recipe that's kept in a safe, and that only family members are ever allowed to become knowledgeable with."

Maria had returned with a small salver on which a few slices of the famous saucisse had been placed.

"I thought you were all out of Duffers?" she said.

"This is the XXXL. It is not for sale. Please," he said, gesturing to the salver.

Odelia speared a slice with the provided toothpick and put it in her mouth. Immediately a strong flavor spread along her palate and her throat, and as she chewed and then swallowed she was struck by the very peculiar taste of the delicacy. Salty with a hint of spice, like a regular salami, and something more. A pleasant aftertaste that was sweet. She frowned as she tried to define it. "Um, vanilla?" she asked. "Or no. Nutmeg?"

Colin smiled. "Well, obviously I can't disclose the exact ingredients, but you are not too far off, Miss Poole. You would make an excellent saucisse taster."

"So how come you ran out of Duffers? Is demand higher than usual?"

"No, we're simply experiencing some production issues. As you might expect, we place the highest demands on the quality of our products, and are currently going through a complete overhaul of our production process. We're building a new plant," he explained when she gave him a curious look. "Demand has increased to such an extent that the old production line simply couldn't keep up. A big part of the process was still done by hand, and unfortunately that wasn't feasible anymore."

"Automation," she said, nodding.

"Indeed. And as our new manufacturing plant goes online, we'll multiply our output. We're selling a lot of sausages through our online store, and hope to expand this. We're also looking into opening stores in other parts of the state, and perhaps even beyond state lines or even internationally. We think we have a fine product, and we're confident the Duffer can compete with any salami out there, whether in the States or in Europe."

"Ambitious plans, Mr. Duffer."

"Well, standing still is the fastest way of moving backward in a rapidly changing world, Miss Poole."

"President Roosevelt?"

"Lauren Bacall. Miss Bacall loved a good sausage."

CHAPTER 19

*A*t the office, Gran was idly leafing through a magazine. She'd been playing Solitaire for a while, then had picked up her phone, only for the darn thing to crash each time she tried to watch one of her favorite shows. So now she had resorted to reading through a copy of *Cosmo* that Tex supplied for his waiting patients, but was quickly bored with the numerous articles about the perfect nails, or how Jennifer Aniston managed to keep looking so young. And just when she was ready to chuck it all and tell Tex she was going home and he could play receptionist himself, the door to the office opened and Scarlett Canyon strode in. "Oh, you gotta be kidding me," muttered Gran. As if she wasn't dealing with enough problems already, Scarlett had to come in and add some more to the pile.

"What do you want?" she asked, none too friendly.

Two more patients sat in the waiting room, and both straightened up with a look of happy anticipation. The whole town knew about the animosity that existed between Scarlett and Vesta, an animosity that spanned decades, and went right back to that one time Vesta had discovered Scarlett, her best friend back then, in the conjugal bed with Vesta's husband Jack, doing the kind of things only married couples are supposed to be doing there. It had been the end of her marriage, and her friendship with Scarlett.

"That's strictly between me and Tex," said Scarlett haughtily. In spite of the fact that she was the exact same age as Vesta, she looked easily two decades younger, and it had cost her a lot of work to make it that way. From her bleached blond hair to her botox-injected forehead to the filler-filled lips and enhanced décolletage, Scarlett still dressed as if she was the blond bombshell that had launched a thousand ships, or at least made a thousand hearts beat faster, and raised the blood pressure of a thousand more.

"As his assistant, it's my duty to ask you to state your business," said Vesta as she brought up Scarlett's file. "So tell me and let's get this over with, shall we?"

"I'm not going to tell you my most intimate, personal secrets," said Scarlett, pressing a shocked hand to her chest. "God knows my complete medical history will be the talk of the town by the time I walk out of Tex's office."

"Are you calling me a gossip?" asked Vesta, narrowing her eyes at the woman.

"I'm calling you a nosy parker. You're not my doctor and I don't have to tell you a damn thing."

"And I'm telling you that you're not going in there until you've stated your business."

Scarlett pressed her lips together. "Oh, yeah? We'll see about that."

Vesta noticed how Scarlett was dressed to impress again. Most patients looked exactly like what they were: sick people, eager to see the medical man and hoping he could make them feel better again. They didn't care what they looked like, and some even showed up dressed in their nightgown, straight out of bed. But not Scarlett, who looked like she was ready to go clubbing, with her deeply cut dress and her shapely legs and her impossibly high heels. Her lips forming a thin line, Vesta moved over to the door that connected the waiting room with Tex's office and positioned herself in front of it.

"You're not going in there until you tell me what you're here for," she snapped.

Scarlett laughed a light laugh that sounded entirely fake. "Oh, Vesta. You're still a hoot, aren't you? Well, all right. If you insist. Now please type all this down in that silly little computer of yours, and don't miss a single word I say. I'm here to see your son-in-law for a new prescription for the pill."

Vesta glowered at her. "The pill my ass. You're too old for the pill."

"You mean *you're* too old for the pill. I'm not. And since I'm sexually very active, I don't want to run the risk of getting pregnant. So that's what I'm here for. Satisfied?"

"You're the exact same age as me," Gran growled.

"I doubt it."

"You're well past the point of hormonal return and you know it. So why don't you tell me what you're really here for and stop jerking me around, will you?"

"I've told you why I'm here. If you can't accept that, for whatever reason, that's not my problem."

"Bullshit," spat Gran, but returned to her desk and started typing anyway. She knew very well that the only thing Scarlett wanted was to get a rise out of her, and she wasn't going to give her the satisfaction. She was going to handle herself like a true professional.

She took a sausage out of her drawer and took a big bite.

A small gasp had her look up. Scarlett had risen from her seat and was standing at the desk.

"Yeah, yeah, yeah, I'm typing, I'm typing," said Gran.

"See?" She turned the screen so Scarlett could follow. "'Here to get a prescription filled for the contraceptive pill, even though she's obviously way too old.'" She noticed Scarlett wasn't listening but intently staring at her sausage. "What?" she asked, annoyed by the woman's weird behavior.

"Is that… a Duffer you got there?" asked Scarlett.

"Yeah, I guess it is," said Gran distractedly. "How do you spell biatch?"

"Lemme have a bite," said Scarlett, licking her lips.

"No, you can't have a bite. That's my damn sausage and you're not coming anywhere near it with that filthy mouth of yours. Who knows where those blowfish lips have been. So is it B-Y-A-T-C-H or B-I-A-T-C-H? Lemme check The Google. The Google knows."

"They're all out of Duffers."

"Who is?"

"Everyone! There are no more Duffers, and they're not coming in until next week."

"So? Wait a week or buy a different brand. Plenty of sausages in the sea. And you should know. You're something of a sausage connoisseur, aren't you? At least that's what you say."

"Oh, you stupid old bat," said Scarlett. "Don't you know the Duffer is the king of saucisse? The tip of the top—top of the heap? There's no saucisse like it. And I have to have a bite. Right now!" And then she grabbed Gran's sausage and put it to her lips!

"Hey, you crazy woman!" Gran yelled, and tried to pry the sausage from Scarlett's lips. It was like pulling a candy cane from a kid.

"One bite!" Scarlett yelled. "I haven't had a Duffer for days!"

"Gimme back my sausage!"

And then Scarlett actually took the sausage and whacked

Gran across the head with it. "Never! Call! The! Duffer! A! Sausage!" she screamed. "It's a saucisse!"

"*My* saucisse!" Gran yelled, and then lunged across the desk for Scarlett.

*W*hen Tex stepped out of his office moments later, attracted by the sounds of a scuffle, he found Scarlett and Vesta on the floor of his waiting room, grappling like a couple of aged wrestlers, and Scarlett beating Vesta with what looked like a sausage.

Shaking his head, he took possession of the object of contention, his gesture drawing howls of rage from both women.

He then took a tentative bite and nodded appreciatively. "Great little sausage."

The next moment something was biting him in the ankle. When he looked down, he saw that it was Scarlett, and then she was screaming. "It's not a sausage! It's a saucisse!"

CHAPTER 20

"We have to get out of here," said Harriet.

"No shit, Sherlock," said Clarice.

"You don't think this is the pound?" asked Dooley.

"No, this is not the pound, Dooley," said Clarice. "And I should know. I've been a frequent resident of that place more times than I care to remember. This is a prison."

"Yeah, this doesn't look like the pound at all," I agreed.

"More like one of those creepy dungeons where serial killers like to collect their victims before they go off and fillet them alive," said Brutus, glancing around.

Harriet shot him a censorious glance. "Nice," she said.

"What?"

"Can't you see that Dooley is terrified?"

We all looked at Dooley, but far from looking terrified he actually seemed excited. He was standing near the far wall, listening intently. We all joined him.

"What's going on?" I asked.

"Listen here, Max," said Dooley, and pointed to a small crack in the wall, where the cement between two bricks had fallen out. So I put my ear to the crack and listened.

"Hey, that sounds a lot like… Uncle Alec!" I said, glancing up at Dooley in surprise.

"I was checking out this wall when suddenly I thought I heard his voice. He must have found this place and come here to get us out. So you see, Max? You were right. Everything is going to be all right after all."

I smiled at Dooley, listening in the meantime, and then my smile disappeared.

"We have to get out of here," Uncle Alec was saying, echoing Harriet's words exactly. "I don't care how, but I have a feeling if we don't escape now, it's going to be too late."

And then another male voice piped up, "You're right, Alec. They're going to kill us if we don't escape."

I abruptly removed my ear from the crack and stared at the others. "Uncle Alec isn't here to save us," I said after a moment. "He's also a prisoner, and is talking about getting killed if he can't escape!"

My statement was met with wails of dismay, and then Harriet was next to press her ear to the wall and listen. After a moment, she nodded. "Max is right. Uncle Alec is a prisoner here, along with a couple of other people whose voices I don't recognize."

"Looks like you were right," Harriet told Clarice. "This is some kind of prison."

"Of course I'm right," Clarice growled. "I've seen enough prisons to know I'm in one, princess."

Harriet frowned, for she hates to be called a princess, except by Brutus. She bit back a sharp retort. This wasn't the time to bicker and fight amongst ourselves. We needed to figure out how to escape this place, or else we might perish, just like Uncle Alec!

So we moved back to the entrance through which we'd dropped down, but as no light came in through there, it was obvious it had been sealed shut by now. And there was still that dog to contend with. There were no windows or other entrances except the one door, but that wasn't a potential avenue of escape either, as it looked very sturdy. I directed my gaze upwards. That red-brick arched ceiling was high and out of reach, although there was a small opening… And that's when an idea struck me.

"Have you ever seen those human pyramids?" I asked.

"The ones where a bunch of people all stand on top of each other?" asked Dooley.

"That's the one. Why don't we try the same, and then one of us slips through that opening up there, and runs home to warn Odelia?"

"Hey, that's a great idea, Max," said Brutus.

I'd recently pulled the same stunt when Dooley and I were locked up in Leonidas Flake's big house, and Dooley had managed to reach an air vent. We'd used plush animals that time. This time we had something even better: real live animals!

"So you go stand over there, Max," said Harriet, immediately taking charge.

"Why do I have to be at the bottom?" I asked. I'd secretly hoped I'd be the one to escape through that hole up there.

"Because you're fat, Max," said Brutus, with his customary lack of tact. "And big fat cats need to be at the bottom, with the lightest ones near the top of the pyramid."

"I'm not fat," I said. "I'm—"

"Yeah, yeah, yeah," said Clarice. "We've heard it all before. Stop arguing, will ya? We don't have time for this nonsense. All fat cats gather over here!" she shouted, and compelled by the sheer force of her personality everyone did as they were told. Soon she and Harriet were working together, herding the others, constructing the pyramid with word and gesture. I was at the lowest rung, as indicated, and even though I said I wasn't feeling well, and had recently undergone an invasive medical procedure, no one paid any mind to my protestations. On top of me stood Brutus, who wasn't big but strong, paws pressing painfully into my neck, and then layer after layer other cats piled on top of that.

I have to say that cats are the perfect creatures to form a pyramid. Humans may be flexible and strong, but cats are even more so. Of course I couldn't see what went on above my head, but as far as I could ascertain things were going swimmingly, as at some point loud cheers rang out and apparently some lucky bastard had managed to reach the top and had escaped through that hole I'd found. I would have pointed out that the credit was all mine, but no one was listening, and besides, by then the weight on my shoulders was such that I was starting to know what a bottom pancake feels like, all the other lucky pancakes piled on top and pushing it down onto its plate. Not a very pleasant sensation!

"Well done, you guys!" said Clarice, clapping her paws. "You can come down now."

Gradually the pyramid was disassembled, and finally I could breathe again.

"Great job, Max," said Brutus, giving me a painful slap on the exact spot where his left paw had made a big impression. I winced.

"So who is the lucky one who made it through?" I asked.

Brutus gave me a confused frown. "Why, don't you know? Dooley, of course. He's the lightest. They elected him unanimously and he heroically accepted to be the messenger."

I gaped at the cat. "Our Dooley?"

"How many other Dooleys do you know, Max? Of course our Dooley."

"But… nobody asked me!"

"It's fine, Max. Dooley will save us all," said Harriet.

"Oh, my," I said, as I plunked down on the dirty, wet floor.

"And what if they catch him? Or what if he gets stuck and can't get out? Or what if—"

But then Harriet placed her paw on mine. "He'll be fine, Max," she said. "Trust me."

I shook my head. I wasn't so sure.

"He'll be fine because he wants us to be fine. He wants you to be fine. His best friend."

I gulped a little. "That's what worries me. That he'll take too many risks, and make the wrong turns, and that I won't be there to help him."

I stared up at the tiny hole, through which my best friend had disappeared. Oh, dear.

CHAPTER 21

Odelia had finally arrived home, after interviewing Colin Duffer, and the moment she walked in she knew something was wrong. Chase was seated on the couch and got up. He had a worried look on his face, and even before he spoke the words she already knew what he was going to say.

"They didn't come home, did they?" she asked, more a statement than a question.

He shook his head. "I'm sorry, honey. I asked your mom and they're not next door either."

"I knew it," she said, sinking down on the couch. "I knew something had happened to them."

"You don't know that. Your cats are smart. They won't allow themselves to be caught by… whoever is doing this."

"Whoever is doing this is out to catch all of Hampton Cove's cats. And if we don't stop them…" She didn't even want to contemplate what this pied piper was planning to do with her cats. "Did you call the pound?"

"One of my officers did. Nothing. And they didn't send out a team today either."

"So it's not the pound. Then who is it?"

"Maybe a person who hates cats? And before you say that people like that don't exist, let me assure you that they do. There's a lot of sick people out there who wouldn't mind hurting poor, innocent animals, just to get a kick out of it. Only last year there was that case of a young guy in Belgium, of all places, who put a kitten in his oven."

"Oh, God. I'm going to be sick."

"Luckily they managed to save the kitten and put the sick bastard behind bars."

"Don't tell me these stories, Chase. You know I can't listen to that stuff."

"We'll find them, and we'll find your uncle, and all the people that have gone missing."

"Do you think the two cases are connected? That someone is kidnapping people and cats?"

"I don't know, babe. It seems very unlikely, though."

Just then, Marge walked in through the sliding glass door. "Have you heard?" she asked.

"About the missing cats? Yeah, we're on it," said Chase.

"Cats? I was talking about your grandmother. She and Scarlett got into a big fight down at the office. Rolling-on-the-floor kind of fight. Scarlett bit your father's ankle."

Odelia stared at her mother as if she'd sprouted a second head. "Scarlett did what?"

"She bit Tex's ankle. He needed disinfecting."

"Is he all right?"

"Oh, he's fine, but she screwed up her dentures."

"Scarlett has dentures?"

"I didn't know either," said Mom. "Oh, here is your grand-mother now."

Tex and Gran walked in, Tex limping, and Gran looking like she won the lottery.

"Have you heard?" she asked, clapping her hands with glee.

"Yeah, you got into a fight," said Odelia.

"Scarlett has dentures! Who knew!"

"By now the whole town, probably," said Mom.

"Are you all right, Dad?" asked Odelia.

"I'll live," said Tex, then showed his battle scars. "She bit really hard. Almost hit bone."

"Yeah, right," said Gran skeptically. "They're dentures, Tex, not vampire's teeth. She didn't even break the skin."

"She did break the skin. Look at those marks!"

"You're such a pussy."

"But why did she bite you?" asked Chase, looking puzzled.

"She tried to grab his sausage," said Gran.

Mom frowned and folded her arms across her chest. "She did what?!"

"It wasn't even my sausage!" said Tex defensively. "It was your mother's, I swear!"

"It was a Duffer," said Gran. "And for some reason Scarlett went nuts when she saw it. Said something about it being the last Duffer in Hampton Cove and if she didn't get a bite she was gonna freak, and then she freaked and bit Tex when he took her Duffer away."

"She probably thought your leg was a Duffer, Tex," said Chase.

"Yeah, yeah, laugh all you want," said Tex, who seemed upset at his bite marks not being appreciated the way he felt they should be. He limped back out of the house.

"He administered himself a tetanus shot, just to be on the safe side," said Gran with a grin, "but when I told him to add a rabies shot he shot down the suggestion, the wimp."

"So what happened to Scarlett?" asked Mom, always the humanist. "Is she all right?"

"Yeah, I guess so," said Gran. "She got her dentures back, that's for sure. And then she waltzed out, but not before taking a big bite out of my Duffer." She showed the Duffer in question, indicating the bite marks where Scarlett had dug her teeth in. "See? Dentures," said Gran triumphantly. "I'll bet nothing about that woman is real."

"So what was that you said about missing cats?" asked Marge.

"Our cats have gone missing," said Odelia. "They're nowhere to be found."

"Yeah, and there's a catnappper going around catnapping cats," Chase added.

"Catnapper my ass," said Gran. "I'll tell you what's going on. I offered those ingrates our special concoction this morning and do you think they said thank you? They refused to eat it! Said they were going on a hunger strike unless I served them up some gourmet soft food instead. So I chucked everything down the garbage disposal and walked off. And now of course they're out there somewhere sulking and complaining to anyone who'll listen that their humans are inhuman and yadda yadda. Always the same story."

Odelia quickly crossed into the kitchen and checked the four bowls. Three of them had been eaten from: Max, Brutus and Dooley's, but not much. "You're probably right, Gran," she said, elation spreading through her like balm. "They must be throwing another one of their temper tantrums and stalked off on a huff as usual."

"Of course! I know those cats. So don't you worry about a thing, honey. They'll be back here tomorrow morning, with their tail between their legs, begging for food. Just you wait and see. Now write this down and write it down exactly as I'm telling you. 'Distinguished medical assistant Vesta Muffin was attacked by well-known looney tunes Scarlett Canyon. Mrs. Canyon, who is seventy-five but claims to be on the pill and sexually active, tried to steal Mrs. Muffin's sausage and when she didn't get what she wanted went nuts and bit Doctor Poole in the ankles. In the process she lost her dentures.' Why aren't you writing? This should all be in your article. Verbatim."

CHAPTER 22

*D*ooley wasn't your typical volunteer. Even though he'd been all in favor of Max's brilliant idea of a cat pyramid, he hadn't envisioned himself in the role of escape artist. And if he'd known his friend would be at the bottom of the pyramid and he at the top, he'd have politely turned down the job. Besides, he was no hero. And even though he'd pointed this out to Clarice, who'd taken charge of the proceedings, she hadn't paid his protestations any mind. She'd simply told him he was the smallest, the lightest, and the only one in his weight class able to communicate with his human, and able to get a message across enemy lines.

So he'd reluctantly agreed in principle, but then the pyramid had been formed and he'd been given a shove in the patootie by Clarice, and before he knew what was happening he was crawling through that opening and now here he was, crawling through this dark and creepy house, in search of the exit.

He was on the ground floor, or so he thought, but as luck would have it he was in a closed room, with no way out. So he'd only gone from one prison to another, and while down below he was with his friends, up here he was all alone. He'd looked down through the hole and could see Max down there. He'd even hollered, but of course they were all chattering so loudly nobody could hear him.

So he'd heaved a deep sigh and had decided that if he was chosen for the part of the hero, he might as well try and play the hero. And so he'd gone in search of the exit. It had taken him several attempts to open the door before he finally discovered a fatal flaw the architect who'd built this place had made: next to the door was a small hole, presumably having served a purpose at some moment in the distant past —possibly a power plug had been placed there, before being stripped by treasure hunters—and so he'd simply clawed away at the thing until the hole was big enough for him to crawl through.

And he'd just managed this daring feat when he smelled sweet victory: a window was open in this next room. So he jumped up onto a rickety old chair, then onto the windowsill, and he was just about to jump through the broken window when he saw that the drop to the ground was a lot longer than he'd anticipated so he balked. No way was he going to make that drop. Plus, there were only brambles down there, and pieces of brick. So even if he survived the drop, his fall wouldn't be a gentle one.

Then again, his friends were in danger, so shouldn't he take the chance? What mattered a few brambles compared to the horrors that awaited his dear friends in that dungeon down below? So he took a deep breath, carefully navigated the broken glass and… took the plunge.

He actually landed pretty well, narrowly missing the brambles. His paws hurt a little, but he was still in one piece, and that's what counted. He raced to a nearby bush, and saw that the van that had brought them was there, just returning with possibly another load of cats, and was now backing up against what he assumed was the hole that led into the scary and smelly dungeon—or cellar.

He slowly backed away from the van, making sure the driver didn't see him, when suddenly someone pinched him and he was picked up by the scruff of his neck.

"And what do we have here?" a rumbling voice said with audible glee.

He protested up a storm, but to no avail. He tried using his claws, but the man held him at some distance, and seemed to enjoy seeing him dangle and claw.

"You're a little fighter, aren't you?" said the man, who was bearded and very big. "Well, let's get you back to where you came from, little buddy."

Just then, though, the man suddenly uttered a loud yelp of pain, and dropped Dooley. And as he was dancing on one leg, grabbing for the other, Dooley heard a sweet, sweet sound: it was Max, and he was screaming, "Let's go, Dooley—run!"

And then he ran, closely followed by Max, right on his tail. In the distance, they could hear the man's dog yapping up a storm, probably unhappy he'd missed this chance.

And they'd been running for what felt like an hour when they finally stopped, hiding by the side of the road. Max was panting heavily, not really built for this kind of strenuous activity, and Dooley cried, "How did you get out?!"

"Clarice scratched the guard," he said between two gasps of breath. "Someone opened the hatch that leads into the basement, and she jumped up and scratched whoever was up there. He vanished from view long enough for me to make my getaway."

"Yeah, I saw that. He arrived to dump a fresh load of cats down the hatch."

"Clarice should have scratched him much, much harder."

"So where is she? And where are the others?"

"He caught her and threw her back into the hole. She sacrificed herself, Dooley, distracting the guy long enough for me to escape. She's a real hero. Just like you."

"Me? You're the hero! You bit that guy, even though you don't have all your teeth!"

"I have to confess it hurts a little," said Max, tentatively moving his jaw. "But I'm not the hero, Dooley. You are. You volunteered to save all of us."

"Actually, Clarice volunteered me."

"Can one cat volunteer another cat? Isn't that a contradiction in terms?"

"I don't know what it is, but that's what she did."

"Whoever volunteered whom, we're out of the dungeon now," he said, patting Dooley on the shoulder. "So let's find Odelia and tell her what's going on before it's too late."

And thus began Max and Dooley's long way home...

CHAPTER 23

O delia and Chase had decided to team up to try and get to the bottom of this missing person business. Three people had gone missing so far, and still they were none the wiser. As far as the missing cat issue was concerned, Odelia was sufficiently satisfied with Gran's explanation about the hunger strike. It sounded exactly like what her cats would do when they didn't get their way. And the fact that a bunch of other people had called in and reported their cats missing didn't necessarily have to mean anything either. Cats were independent creatures, and liked to roam around, wild and free, until they got hungry and returned to the safety of home, hearth, and food bowl.

Joining them for their investigation was Gran, of course, who felt she needed to make a contribution, and who was feeling on top of her game after her tussle with Scarlett.

"Slow the car, Chase," said Gran suddenly, and cranked down her window. "Hey!" she yelled. "Hey, you! Yeah, I'm talking to you, cats!"

Two cats were walking down the sidewalk, surprised that a human would address them.

"Have you by any chance seen my cats?" Gran asked. "Their names are Max, Dooley, Harriet and Brutus. Max is big and orange, Dooley small and gray, Harriet is a white Persian and Brutus is butch and black. No? Okay, carry on, fellas."

She retracted her head, allowing the cats to continue their journey, but then changed her mind and stuck her head out once more. "Hey! cats!"

The cats halted once again.

"A bunch of cats seem to have gone missing. Any idea where they might have gone off to? No? Ok, fine. Be that way."

"Come on, Gran," said Odelia with light reproach. "They can't help it that they haven't seen Max and the others."

"Well, they should. If cats don't look out for each other, who will?"

They continued their journey, and Chase said, "I'm sure they're fine."

"Oh, sure," said Gran. "Just thought I'd ask, just to be on the safe side."

They'd arrived at the house of one of the youngest lottery winners in the nation's history, and Odelia thought it didn't look like the house of a lottery winner at all. It was a modest little villa that seemed to date back to the seventies, and was slightly run down.

They got out and walked up the short drive to the front door, Chase taking out his police badge and Gran putting on her game face, which apparently consisted of her knitting her brows and dragging down the corners of her mouth, giving her a bulldog look. Chase pressed his finger to the buzzer and moments later a mousy-looking woman appeared. She'd obviously been crying, for her eyes were red-rimmed. Unless she'd been peeling onions she was prob-ably upset over her missing son.

"Mrs. Pope?" said Chase, holding up his badge. "My name is Chase Kingsley. I'm with the Hampton Cove Police Department. And this is Odelia Poole, civilian consultant, and Vesta Muffin, um, also a, um, civilian consultant."

"I'm a private dick," Gran explained. "But I work with our local boys and girls in blue from time to time. When they're completely stuck, that's when they come knocking on my door."

"Oh," said the woman, looking a little confused. "Well, come in. One of your colleagues was here yesterday, and told me to wait another twenty-four hours before, um…"

"Yes, I'm very sorry about that," said Chase. "But it now appears that your son's disappearance is part of a bigger story. Several people have gone missing now."

"And a ton of cats," said Gran, "but we're not worried about that, cats being cats."

"Exactly," said Chase, giving Gran a critical glance. Even though the cop was now accustomed to Odelia accompanying him on his investigations, the addition of her grandmother was a more recent development he still needed to wrap his head around.

They followed Mrs. Pope into the living room and took a seat at the table.

"So can you tell me what happened, Mrs. Pope?" asked Odelia, taking out her trusty little notebook just as Chase took out his.

Gran, meanwhile, seeing her two colleagues armed with pen and paper, seemed annoyed that she wasn't as well-equipped as they were, so she took out a puzzle book from her purse, a chewed-up pencil, and started scribbling in the margins.

"Well, as I told your colleague yesterday, Elon recently won the lottery, and he hasn't stopped partying since, buying all of his friends, the old ones and the new ones, drinks at his favorite club, clubbing every night. So I told him the night before last that he couldn't take the car—I wasn't going to allow him—since he only got this license last month and he practically totaled one of his cars by driving it into a lamp-post last week. Of course he wouldn't listen, and it was only when his sister Marcie turned it into a bet about the environment that he took his bike…"

She sniffed audibly, and dragged a couple of paper napkins from a dispenser and pressed them to her nose and eyes. A tall man with a distinct stoop had walked in from the kitchen and took a seat next to Mrs. Pope. Judging from the picture frames on the mantel he was the missing boy's father, and now placed his arm around his wife's shoulder. He looked pale as a ghost, dark rings under his eyes. "Do you have any news about our boy?" he asked.

"No news, I'm afraid," said Odelia kindly. "But we're doing everything we can to find him."

"So he took his bike, and where did he go?" asked Chase.

"Not far," said Mr. Pope, clearing his throat. "Just into town. He was going to the Café Baron, for a party in his honor. He's been partying non-stop since he won the lottery."

"How much did he win?" asked Gran.

"Um, three hundred and twenty million."

"Wow, that's a lot of money."

"At the rate he's been spending it, I'm afraid it will be gone soon," said Mrs. Pope.

"He's already bought himself a Lamborghini and a Maserati and one of them electric cars," said Mr. Pope. "A Tesla. And a new house for us, a house for his sister, one for his grandmother, a house for his aunt and uncle, one for his niece, one for his best friend…"

"That's a lot of houses," said Chase with a smile.

"He's obviously trying to spread the wealth around," Odelia added.

"He's a good boy," his mother agreed, taking another tissue from the box and pressing it to her nose. "Other kids would probably buy themselves a fancy condo and go and live with some supermodel celebrity influencer they met at a party but not my Elon."

"Only problem is, he's too nice—too kind," said his father.

"Elon has a good heart—that's how we raised him."

"So he's been buying gifts for all of his friends, and suddenly he's found so many new friends it's hard to keep up. The money's been flowing like water, and I think that must be what happened. One of his new friends must have decided to take advantage of our boy's generosity and must have wanted more than Elon was willing to give. So they must have gotten into a fight and…"

"Don't say that, Mike," said the boy's mother. "Let's not get ahead of ourselves."

"You should talk to those boys," said Mike. "They'll be able to tell you what happened."

"What do you think happened, Mrs. Pope?" asked Odelia.

"I think Elon had one too many, and rode his bike into a ditch and that's where he still is."

"Even if that were true, he would have woken up by now," said her husband.

"Not if he hit his head. You need to send out a search party, Detective Kingsley."

"We already tried that, though, didn't we, Marcia?" said the husband.

"Tried what?" asked Odelia.

"We called all of his friends, and according to everyone we spoke to the last place Elon was seen was the Café Baron. So we walked the distance from the club back to the house… checking all the ditches… and…" She sniffed.

"And nothing," said Mike. "Not a trace of him anywhere along that stretch of road."

Odelia nodded as she jotted down a note.

"Please find my boy," said Marcia. "He's a good boy, with a big heart. If he's in a ditch somewhere, we need to find him before… before…" She broke down in tears.

Once they were outside again, Gran said, "Poor woman. I can't imagine what it must be like to have your son suddenly go missing like that."

"Your son has suddenly gone missing," Chase pointed out.

"No, he hasn't. Alec is probably off somewhere on a toot. Or maybe he met that Tracy Sting he likes so much and they're off to the Adirondacks again, just like the last time."

"He wouldn't do that without letting us know," said Odelia.

"Like hell he wouldn't. You don't know Alec."

"Actually, we do," Chase pointed out.

"That's my theory and I'm sticking to it," said Gran stubbornly.

"So has the officer who was here yesterday retraced Elon's steps?" asked Odelia.

"Yeah, she did this morning, but found no trace of him, just like Mike and Marcia said."

"So weird," said Odelia, "for a bunch of people all to go missing around the same time."

"You know what this is, right?" said Gran as they filed back into Chase's pickup.

"No, I don't," said Chase. "But I'm sure you will enlighten us." He was not a big fan of Gran's crazy theories.

"Aliens," said Gran as she buckled up. "Aliens must have come down and landed in that terrible storm we had the other night, and we all know what those aliens are like."

"Um, no, we don't," said Chase tentatively.

"They kidnap people! That's what they do. Abduct them

in their big spaceships so they can do all kinds of weird experiments. And they must have decided one wasn't enough, so they kidnapped the August kid, too. Mark my words. It's those nasty aliens."

As interesting as Gran's theory might be, though, Odelia thought something else was going on here, and she was convinced her uncle Alec had been taken, too.

And not by aliens. Or by Tracy Sting.

CHAPTER 24

"*I* don't care what you say, I'm not sleeping next to that woman again," said Tex.

"You don't have to sleep with her," said Marge as she peeled another potato. "If you make peace with her she can go back to her room, and Odelia can have her house back."

"Make peace with her! Easier said than done. How do you suggest I pull off a miracle like that?"

"You need to figure out some kind of compromise, Tex."

They were in the kitchen, and Marge was glad that Odelia and Chase had decided to take her mother along for their investigation so she and Tex could have this little chat.

"Look, you have to dig a little deeper. Try to figure out what's really going on here."

"What's going on is that your mother hates her job. She wants to stay home and watch TV instead of being cooped up in that office handling my patients all day long."

"No, that's where you're wrong. Vesta loves to socialize, and she loves being a doctor's assistant. It gives her prestige, and she enjoys being in the thick of things."

"But she wants to watch her shows. Says sitting at that

desk is killing her. Too boring. Unless Scarlett Canyon drops by, of course," he added with a grin, "to spice things up."

"Why don't we buy her a tablet computer? That way she can watch all the shows she wants, and surf the web, or play computer games, and it won't set us back two thousand bucks."

Tex tapped the table. "She seems to have her mind set on this foldable phone."

"I think that's just her opening bid. Pretty sure she'll settle for a brand-new iPad."

"How about a second-hand iPad?"

"Tex," said Marge warningly.

"Look, what she should be doing is work," he said, as he sniffed at a sausage he'd taken from the fridge. "She should be greeting my patients and answering the phone. What will people think when my receptionist is watching *Days of Our Lives* and *General Hospital* all day long? Word will spread and soon people will stop coming."

"They won't stop coming because you're the only decent doctor in town."

"There are other towns, honey, and there's the clinic. People don't have to come to me, you know. They can take their hernias and their ingrowing toenails to Denby Jennsen over in Happy Bays, or Cary Horsfield in Hampton Keys. And once I've lost all my patients, then what? We'll have to sell the house and move to a town where nobody knows me or my lousy reputation and start all over again. Or take over an existing practice in Utah or Colorado or Alaska or work for another doctor as his apprentice. I'm too old to be an apprentice, Marge—or to start all over again from scratch."

"Oh, don't be such a drama queen," said Marge as she put the pot with the potatoes on the stove. It was a Berghoff pot, one of a set she was very fond of.

"I'm not being a drama queen! Remember what she did

today? Got into a fight with Scarlett over a sausage! A stupid sausage!"

Marge cast a quick glance at the sausage her husband was waving. "Oh, there's that Duffer. I knew we had one left."

"Yeah, I keep them at the back of the fridge where Vesta won't find them. She's like a rabid dog when she sees them. Attacks without provocation. Just like her crazy friend."

"I don't think she'll like it when you call Scarlett her friend, honey," said Marge as she glanced out the kitchen window into the backyard. Odd that the cats were nowhere to be found. Usually around dinner time you couldn't keep them away, as there was always something that fell off the table when their family sat down for dinner. She remembered Vesta's words about that hunger strike. Knowing her cats they wouldn't last a day without food. She smiled and took the pork chops from the fridge. They'd be back soon.

"What's the deal between those two anyway?" asked Tex as he cut a slice off the Duffer and took a bite.

"Oh, you know," said Marge.

"I know what happened way back when," he said. "But why are they still at each other's throats? Your dad is long gone, so there's no reason for them to be enemies."

"Vesta likes to hold a grudge. And so does Scarlett. She's not the innocent bystander in this."

"So maybe you should try and negotiate a truce?"

She made a scoffing sound. "No way. I don't want to be torn limb from limb by a pack of rabid old ladies. They're vicious."

"And don't I know it," he said, massaging his ankle.

"You wanna know what I think? I think they like this feud. It adds spice to their lives." She moved over to where her husband sat and put a slice of Duffer into her mouth. The meat simply melted on her tongue. "Oh, my God. What do they put in these things?"

"Delicious, huh?"

"Incredible."

"At least the Duffers managed to put this town on the map."

"You know?" she said, suddenly feeling magnanimous. "Why don't we give my mother exactly what she wants?"

"You mean, buy her one of those foldable smartphones?"

"Yeah. I mean, why not? She's getting on, and she won't be with us forever. And it's not as if we can't afford one, right?"

"Right," said Tex dubiously. He put another piece of Duffer into his mouth. "I guess we could always sell her old phone, and then add a little extra and buy her a new one."

Marge sat down on her husband's lap and gave him a kiss. "And then you will finally be able to sleep with your wife again."

"Finally," he said with a smile.

She returned the smile. "You're the best hubby in the whole wide world, have I ever told you that? And I'm a very lucky girl."

"You've told me, but it never hurts to hear it again," said Tex, then took another slice and tore it into two pieces, popped one into his mouth and the other one into Marge's.

"Oh, my God," she murmured, and gave him another kiss, then lingered. "The house is ours, hubby," she said hoarsely. "The kids are away, my mom is away, and so are the cats."

"Are you thinking what I'm thinking, wifey?"

She giggled, and then Mr. and Mrs. Poole were scooting up the stairs.

❧

Chase drove the car into town, and they happened to pass by the Duffer Store. A mass of people had gathered on the sidewalk, and they were shouting something.

"What's going on over there?" asked Chase.

"Disgruntled customers, probably," said Odelia.

"Let's check it out," said Chase as he parked across the road. He got out and rolled his shoulders, then marched in the direction of the protestors.

"I love it when he does that, don't you?" said Gran.

"Does what?" asked Odelia, wondering what was up with all this Duffer mania.

"He assumes the cop stance."

"The cop stance?" said Odelia with a laugh.

"Sure! He straightens his shoulders, lifts his chin, plasters this fierce expression on his face and dives right in. The cop stance! Just like putting on the uniform. And then when he gets home at night, he takes it off, drapes it across the back of the chair and he's Chase Kingsley again, son, husband… father."

"I never thought about it like that," said Odelia, though she had to admit there was some truth to what her grandmother was saying.

"All cops do that," said Gran, as if she was the world expert on cops. "It's a part they play, a role they assume, and like any actor they slip in and out of it. Like Robert de Niro or Al Pacino. They become the mobsters they're playing, and Chase becomes the cop."

"Well, I don't think he sees it that way," said Odelia, "but he probably does have to project a certain authority when he approaches a mob scene like that."

The commotion was still in full swing, and she now wondered if Chase needed backup.

"It's because they ran out of Duffers," said Gran.

"Yeah, I know. I interviewed Colin Duffer this afternoon. They should have fresh Duffers soon. They've been working on an entirely new production facility."

"Great. I like my Duffers."

"Everybody likes their Duffers." Except for her, though now that she'd tasted one she agreed they were pretty yummy.

Chase came walking back to the car again. His hair was a little mussed, his cheeks were flushed, and he had a hunted look in his eyes. When he dropped down in the driver's seat he blew out a deep breath. "These people are crazy."

"What's going on?" asked Odelia.

"They're picketing the Duffer Store!"

"And what are their demands?"

"Duffers!" he said as he started up the car. "The Duffer Store ran out of Duffers and they're not happy. I managed to get in and talk to Colin Duffer and he told me that if this keeps up he will have to close down the store. He asked me to get rid of these protestors. Arrest them if I have to."

"Oh, my God!" said Odelia. "No way."

"Yeah, I told him to talk to the Mayor. Though the best thing he can do is close up for now and get cracking on a fresh batch of Duffers. That's the only thing that's going to make those people go away. But he says that if he closes now he might never reopen."

"He's got a point," said Odelia. "People may be clamoring for Duffers now, but next month there will be some new thing, and Duffers will be the last thing people want."

"I don't think so," said Chase. "These sausages are pretty popular."

"Tell me about it," said Gran, who'd taken her half-eaten Duffer out of her purse again and now took a big bite.

Suddenly, there was a shout outside, and Odelia saw how a woman stood looking in through the car window at Gran's Duffer.

"SHE'S GOT A DUFFER!" the woman screamed. Immediately the rest of the mob crossed the street, and they all converged on the car, pounding the windows to get in.

146

"Christ, I feel like I'm in a zombie movie," said Gran.

"Better get us out of here, Chase," said Odelia.

"Yeah, before they grab me and my Duffer!"

Chase put the car in gear, and before people could break down the windows and drag Gran bodily out of the car, he was moving away from the curb, careful not to run over anyone's toes, and then they were finally mobile again.

"Phew!" said Gran. "Did you see that? What's gotten into people?!"

"I don't know," said Odelia, looking back at the mob scene. "But it's not good."

At least she had another angle for her next article. Duffer Mania!

CHAPTER 25

*W*e'd been walking for what felt like miles, when finally we found ourselves on familiar terrain. We'd passed the park where cat choir holds its nightly rehearsals, and it struck me how devoid of feline life it was. Usually the park is teeming with cats, even during the daytime, but especially at night, of course. Now there wasn't a single cat in sight. In fact I didn't think we'd met a fellow feline all along the road into town.

"All cats are at the monster house," said Dooley.

"Yeah, looks like," I agreed.

"Too bad cats don't use smartphones, huh, Max?" he said. "We could have called Odelia by now, and told her what's going on, and she could have come to our rescue."

"Yeah, too bad," I said. Then again, where would we put it? It's not as if cats have pockets, or carry backpacks. We're unencumbered by the trappings of modern life, and that's just fine with me. So what if we don't have smartphones? Who needs a smartphone anyway? Just to be bothered every second of every day by those weird beeps and buzzes. I think

I'd go nuts if I had to carry one of those annoying little devices.

"If I had a smartphone I'd make Odelia my screensaver," said Dooley, still dreaming.

"We should have seen her by now," I said. "Odelia and I are very much attuned. Usually when we're in trouble she senses it, and manages to find us all on her own."

"Maybe she's distracted," said Dooley.

"Yeah, could be." I myself was distracted by the pain in my jaw. That operation had done more damage than I'd anticipated, and now with being catnapped and all, I hadn't been able to take my medication, and the pain in my gums was frankly killing me.

"You don't look so good, Max," said Dooley, who'd noticed I wasn't at my best.

"It's my teeth. They hurt."

"But I thought Vena pulled your teeth?"

"She did."

"So if they're not there anymore, how can they hurt?"

"I don't know, Dooley. All I know is that they hurt."

"Phantom pain," said Dooley knowingly. "I saw it on the Discovery Channel. It's when a body part that was removed still hurts. You are still attached to your teeth, Max. Time to let go."

Easier said than done. I liked my teeth, and hadn't been ready to have them removed.

"We're almost there," I said. "And then this ordeal will finally be over."

And we'd just reached Harrington Street and turned the corner, when suddenly there was a screech of brakes, and before we had the chance to react a net was thrown over the both of us, and we were scooped up and deposited back into that same horrible van!

"Oh, no!" cried Dooley. "I can't believe they caught us again!"

The man slammed the door, and there we were, once again: surrounded by a sea of cats. Talk about déjà-vu!

"We have to escape, you guys," said Dooley, addressing the other cats. "They're taking us to a dungeon, and once we're in there there will be no escape!"

"And how would you know?" asked a familiar-looking cat. I quickly recognized him as Milo, who'd once been a guest at our house, and belonged to one of Odelia's neighbors.

"Because we've been there, Milo," I said. "Literally."

"Yeah, we just escaped from the dungeon and walked all the way back here to warn Odelia, only to get captured again the moment we turned into our street!" said Dooley.

"So you're telling us you were caught before, managed to escape this inescapable dungeon, and now you're caught again?" He was giving us a mocking smile. "Sounds like a very likely story, right, fellas?"

"Yeah, very likely," said a scruffy-looking cat with a scar over his right eye.

"But it's all true! We have to escape now, or it will be too late!" said Dooley.

"Yeah, right," said Milo. "And I'm a messenger from the planet Zortaugh and I'm here to bring you all everlasting peace, prosperity and all the cat kibble you'll ever need."

There were loud laughs at that one.

"No, I think what's more likely is that you don't like being caught, and you're inventing stories to make yourselves look like the heroes," said Milo.

"Dooley is telling the truth," I said. "Practically all the cats of Hampton Cove are in that dungeon, and so is Chief Alec, along with other humans, and they're all locked up."

"Oh, so the chief of police is a prisoner, too, huh? This story just keeps getting better and better!"

"You have to believe us, Milo!"

"Oh, Maxie, Maxie," said Milo, shaking his head. "I've always known you were something of a fantasist, but it's sad to see you've started believing your own lies now."

"Coming from a true fantasist that's high praise," I said, getting a little annoyed.

"Me? When have I ever made up a story? Never. So who's the fantasist now?"

"So what is your explanation then? Why are we here? And where are they taking us?"

Milo shrugged. "It's obvious, isn't it? We've all been selected by The Cat Snax Company for the introduction of their new and improved formula. A special treat."

"Yeah, we're the lucky ones," said another cat.

"You really think The Cat Snax Company is organizing this trip?"

"Of course! And I love it! I don't know about you guys, but I feel truly blessed."

"I'll bet they're taking us to Las Vegas," said a short, red cat. "I love Vegas."

"I think it's the Bahamas," said the scruffy cat. "Get ready for sun and surf, you guys."

"This isn't the airport shuttle bus!" I said.

"Yes, and we should know," said Dooley. "We were on an airport shuttle bus when Odelia flew us all to England on Prince Dante's private jet to meet Tessa Torrance."

"Ooh, you were flown to England on Prince Dante's private jet," said Milo. "Aren't you the lucky snowflakes. Don't tell me you met the Queen?"

"And her corgis!" said the red cat, to everyone's hilarity.

"How did you know?" said Dooley. "They were very nice, the Queen's corgis. Well, not at first, of course, but once we

151

got to know them better, Sweetie, Fräulein and Molly were really charming. They even warned us about the pins on those PBEs we got—PBE stands for Pet of the Order of the British Empire—the Queen gave them to us. But she didn't use pins on us, of course. Her Majesty used nice ribbons. Very considerate. And painless."

"I don't see any ribbons around your necks," said Milo. "Do you see any ribbons, guys?"

"No, we don't," said the red cat. "And not a trace of those PFCs either."

"PBEs," Dooley corrected him. "PBE stands for—"

"So I'll bet you met the President of the United States, too, huh?" said Milo. "Oh, and the Pope, of course. In fact Odelia probably flies you around the world in your private jet so you two can meet all kinds of famous people. Rock stars, movie stars… pet stars."

"Well, actually…" Dooley began, but I interrupted him.

"Forget it, Dooley," I said. "Don't you see he's simply making fun of us?"

"He is?" said Dooley, sounding surprised.

I decided to leave Milo and his cronies to their Cat Snax Vegas dreams, and retreated into a corner of the van to confer with my friend.

"We have to escape, Dooley," I said. "Once we're inside that dungeon, our chances of escaping again will be slim to non-existent."

"We could always try the cat pyramid again," he suggested.

"We could, but they might be more vigilant now, and won't let us trick them so easily."

We searched around for an avenue of escape, but the van was obviously built to keep us in, not allow us to slip out.

"We have to be on our toes, Dooley," I said. "Keep our eyes

peeled. And the first chance we get we make a run for it, all right? We don't hesitate, we run like the wind."

"Like the wind, Max," he said, a determined look on his furry face.

"Oh, one question, guys," said Milo, who'd been entertaining the group at our expense. "Is it true that you met Bigfoot? Abominable Snowman? The Loch Ness Monster? Or is that just a rumor floating around? Help me clear this up. It's important."

More laughter ensued, and Dooley and I shook our heads at so much ignorance.

Dooley was on his toes, though. Literally. Ready to escape.

CHAPTER 26

"It's all my fault, lieutenant!" the woman was saying. Lenora Balk was blond and probably a beauty, Odelia thought, though at the moment it was hard to be sure. Her face was red from crying, and her hair was a mess. She was very busty, though, which might explain the attraction Hank the traveling salesman must have experienced when he'd offered her Berghoff pots and pans and in return had gotten more than he bargained for.

"I'm sure your husband will turn up soon enough," said Chase. "He's probably hiding out in some sleazy motel somewhere, and doesn't want to answer your calls."

"But that's just the thing, captain. He never switches off his phone. And he always picks up when I call, even when we're in a fight."

"Yeah, but this was more than just a fight, though, right?" said Chase, who, as usual, had taken the lead. The man was aces at putting people at their ease, Odelia thought.

"Well…" said Lenora, casting down her eyes.

"You mean this wasn't the first time?" asked Odelia.

"It was the first time he caught me, if that's what you

mean," said Lenora, flashing her lashes. "You see, I had an affair with our neighbor last year? And Bertie found out about it when Rick—that's our neighbor—sent me a picture of his… well, let's just say it was all Bertie needed to figure out something untoward was going on, if you see what I mean."

"And how did he figure that?" asked Gran, who'd suddenly taken an interest in the proceedings. Until then, she'd been nodding along, but now really perked up.

"Well, obviously Bertie would never send a picture of his thing to himself," said Lenora, looking slightly flustered.

"You mean your neighbor Rick sent the picture to your husband's phone?" said Gran, her eyes sparkling with excitement. This was more the kind of stuff she liked.

"Yeah, he must have gotten his wires crossed or something. He used to text Bertie all the time, they were good friends—well, we were all good friends, me and Bertie and Rickie and Rickie's wife Francine. So when Bertie got the picture of Rickie's thing he wasn't happy. In fact he was pretty upset."

"So how did Bertie know that Rickie's picture was meant for you?" asked Gran, delving deeper into the subject.

"Because of the caption," said the woman.

"The caption?"

Lenora looked pained. "Do I have to tell you? I don't think this is relevant, captain."

"Detective," Chase corrected her. "Just tell us, please, Mrs. Pope."

"Oh, all right. Rickie added the message 'Soon in a Jacuzzi near you.' Because he has a Jacuzzi, see. And we liked to do it in the Jacuzzi when Bertie was away. And then he also added 'When will that moron of a husband of yours be back?' That's when Bertie really got upset. He thought Rickie was his friend, and friends don't call their friends morons."

Or canoodle with their wives in the Jacuzzi when they're away, Odelia thought. "And he didn't walk out on you that time?" she asked, surprised at this Bertie's loyalty.

"No, he didn't, Miss Poole. He sat me down that time and told me he was very cross with me. And I told him he had good reason to be, and that I'd never set foot in Rickie's Jacuzzi ever again. I also told Rickie to apologize to Bertie for calling him a moron and he did and that was that. Or at least I thought it was. And then all of a sudden he walks out and disappears on me. So I simply know something bad happened to him, sheriff."

"Detective," Chase said, scratching his head. "It seems like a plausible response from your husband to walk out on you after he caught you with…" He consulted his notes. "Hank, is it?"

"Probably," the woman agreed. "He sold me some very nice Berghoff pots."

"That was very considerate of him," said Gran with a grin.

"Bertie would never walk out on me, sergeant," said Lenora. "My daddy walked out on my mommy when I was a little girl, and it was a very traumatizing experience, so I made Bertie promise never to pull a stunt like that. So I know that something terrible must have happened to him, so please, please, please find him for me, commander."

"Detective," Chase corrected her.

She nodded, then attached herself to Chase's left bicep, squeezing it and flashing her eyelashes once more. "Please find my husband for me, Chief Chase. I know I treated him horribly, and I know I don't deserve a good man like Bertie, but I want him back. Those other guys, that's just sex, you see, but my Bertie, that's… well, I do love him, you see."

And oddly enough, Odelia actually believed her when she said it.

Later, when they were back in the car, Gran said, "I don't

156

believe for a moment that guy was abducted, like his wife seems to think. He simply walked out when he saw her with that guy and now he's probably drowning his misery in some dive bar in Mexico."

"Possible," Chase agreed.

"I don't know," said Odelia. "I think she wasn't lying when she said she loves her husband."

"She has a funny way of showing it," Gran grunted.

"If he loves her back it's all the more reason for him to walk out on her," Chase said.

"I don't know," said Odelia. "There's something funny going on. What are the odds of two people to go missing in the space of two days? Very slim, I should say."

"Three people," said Gran. "You forgot about the little boy."

"Four, if you add Chief Alec," said Chase.

Odelia took out her phone and tried her uncle's cell again. Straight to voicemail, just like all the previous times she'd tried him. So if he had been abducted by aliens, which seemed to be Gran's grand theory, the aliens weren't picking up the phone either.

They'd arrived at the house where the August family lived, and Gran had taken her Duffer out of her purse and was munching on it again. "Want a bite?" she asked.

"No, thanks," said Odelia.

They rang the bell, and after the requisite introductions, they were invited in. The August home was a modest one-story structure, and judging from the stack of Missing Person flyers in the hallway, and people coming and going to pick them up, the search for the missing boy was in full swing. They took a seat in the living room, and while Chase made the introductions, Odelia picked up a flyer and studied the kid's face. Nicky August looked about eight, with a gap-toothed smile and a freckled nose. She felt her heart sink at the thought of what could possibly have happened to him.

"If I told him once, I told him a million times," said Alma, the boy's mother. "Never stray too far from home. But you know what boys are like. They get caught up in whatever game they're playing, and before you know it they're out on the street, chasing a ball, or chasing a car, thinking they're Superman or Batman or whatever."

"So he was playing in the backyard…" Chase prompted, jotting down notes.

"He and Jay were kicking the ball around, and then next thing I know I look through the kitchen window and they're gone. For a moment I simply couldn't breathe. You can't imagine what it feels like, Detective. One moment they were there, and the next… poof! Gone! I looked everywhere, and when I didn't see them of course I ran into the street, and then rang the neighbors' house and the house across the street and all the other houses but no one had seen them. They had simply vanished. Like smoke."

"No cars that you thought looked suspicious?" asked Chase. "Or someone driving past the house the last couple of days that you never saw before in the neighborhood?"

"No, nothing like that," said the woman's husband Mark.

"You said he was playing with… Jay?" asked Odelia with a frown. "So who's Jay?"

"Oh, Jay is Nicky's best friend," said Alma. "They've been besties since first grade. Always together. We're very lucky that Nicky found a good friend like him, because in kindergarten he wasn't very social, and never really bonded with anyone."

"Nicky is a single child, you see," said Mark. "After we had him, we tried but…"

"He was a miracle baby," said Alma. "I didn't even think I could get pregnant. The doctors had told us to stop trying, and maybe adopt, so when I got pregnant it took me a while to realize what was happening, and so when Nicky was born we were both over the moon, of course. We tried for a second one, but I guess one miracle was enough."

"So that's why we were so happy when Nicky found Jay. He's like the brother he never had. Always together, never a cross word."

"But… we haven't received a report about a Jay missing," said Chase.

"Probably because Jay's folks are out of town," said Alma.

"When they're away—and they often are—Jay stays with his aunt," said Mark.

"We called her last night, to tell her about what happened, but she didn't seem overly concerned."

"She seems to think Nicky and Jay ran into town to go to the movies or to the mall."

"We told her Nicky wouldn't do that. He wouldn't just go off on his own. But she laughed and said we didn't know Nicky as well as she did, and then hung up on us."

"So there's another little boy missing, and we weren't even told?" said Chase with a frown.

"Is it possible that they did go into town?" asked Gran. "That they did go to the movies? Boys being boys, I mean."

Both parents shook their heads decidedly. "No way," said Alma. "Nicky knows not to do that."

"We've always been very protective of him," Mark explained.

"Maybe a little overprotective," Nicky's mother added.

"We were so happy when we had him, and also afraid of losing him, that he knows not to run off without telling us and scaring us half to death in the process."

"No, ma'am," said Alma decidedly. "Someone took our boy. Just took him like that."

CHAPTER 27

*C*olin Duffer watched the angry crowd that had gathered outside his shop with concern. He didn't like the crowd, even though he knew he should. The crowd irked him, but at the same time the crowd also showed that their strategy, once deemed so risky and outrageous, had won through to success in spite of the odds.

"I hate those people," he said.

His brother, watching the mob scene with an air of detachment, retorted, "Don't hate them. Love them. They are our customers, Colin. Our hapless, dimwitted customers, and they're all crazy about our product."

"Yeah, so crazy that they're about to knock out our windows and drag us out into the street so they can beat us up."

"Nah, they'll never go that far. Though it would be a testament to their enthusiasm for the Duffer."

Colin sighed. "You do realize we're losing money, don't you? And not making it?"

"As soon as we're fully stocked on Duffers again we'll be swimming in cash, buddy. It'll be like printing money, and we don't even have to go through the tedious process of installing a printing press and becoming counterfeiters. All we have to do is create more Duffers. Easy as pie. Or sausage."

"So what's taking so long?"

"Technical issues. Our technicians are working on it. When you move to a fully automated production process there's always kinks to be ironed out at first. But as soon as everything is up to speed we'll be able to crank out twice as many Duffers as before."

"We should never have built that new plant," Colin grumbled. "We were doing fine."

"You can't stop progress, little brother. Or have you forgotten about the Chinese?"

"Setting up a production line in China shouldn't pose a problem," Colin admitted.

"Though we'll have to tweak the formula, of course."

"Of course," Colin agreed.

"We did a blind taste test in Beijing last week."

"And?"

"They loved it! Absolutely loved the Duffer!"

"Do you think we could try the Chinese formula over here?"

"Why not? But let's not get ahead of ourselves. Let's stick to the tried and true for now."

"For now," Colin agreed. They both stared at the seething masses protesting on the sidewalk, then Colin said, "Did I tell you that a reporter dropped by the house earlier?"

"No, you didn't. What did she want?"

"Oh, the usual. The history of the Duffer, for a puff piece in the *Gazette*."

"Soon there will be puff pieces in the *Times*, *Good House-keeping*, *USA Today*…"

"Do you really think all this exposure is a good idea?"

"A good idea! It's free publicity, bro. And besides, all publicity is good publicity. So keep the bloodhounds from the press coming, and we'll keep serving them Duffers."

But as Colin watched the mob shouting slogans about bringing the Duffer back, he couldn't help experiencing those niggling doubts playing havoc with his nervous system.

Chris might be the glass-half-full kind of guy, but he wasn't. He also knew the tremendous risks they had taken—and were still taking. Then again, every successful business person took risks. Their father had taken the same risks, and their grandfather before him. Their current risks might be a little bigger than theirs, but the rewards they'd reap would have made papa and grandpapa proud. At least if they managed to get the new Duffer into stores. If not, that mob would destroy them as soon as praise them.

*U*ncle Alec opened his eyes. He discovered to his surprise that he'd fallen asleep. He'd been lying on his side on the hard floor and had been sure he'd never be able to find sleep, but somehow his tired body had taken over and shut down for a refreshing nap.

He didn't feel all that refreshed, though. More as if he'd been put on the rack. He got up and stretched his sore limbs, and saw that Elon in the cell across from him had the same idea.

"And?" Elon asked, a vague hope in his voice. "Any ideas on how to get us out of here?"

"None," said Alec.

"Hey, you're the chief of police, man. You're paid to come up with ideas."

"Well, I'm sorry to say I'm not a professional escape artist, all right?"

"You don't have to bite my nose off. I'm just saying. If you can't get us out of here, who can? I'm just a shelf stacker who got lucky and won Mega Millions." He glanced over to the third prisoner, still tucked away in his cell right next to Alec.

"Don't look at me," Bertie grumbled. "I'm just an insurance broker who got unlucky when his wife decided to favor a hairy bald traveling salesman over her husband."

In spite of their predicament, Alec laughed. "How can a man be hairy and bald at the same time?"

"Trust me, it's possible," grunted Bertie.

They were all silent for a beat, and Alec frowned when he focused on the noise that seemed to be coming from behind the door to his left. "Do you guys hear that?" he asked.

"Sounds like cats," said Elon.

"Yeah, cats," Alec confirmed. "And a lot of them."

Suddenly a bear of a man wearing a mask passed by their cells, put his ear to the door where the caterwauling was coming from, then pounded the door with his fist. "Shut up, you stupid creatures!" The cats ignored his instructions, for the caterwauling continued in full force. "Stupid animals," the man muttered, then gave the door a kick with his booted foot for good measure and walked away.

"Hey, buddy," said Elon. "How long are you going to keep us down here?"

"Yeah, I'm hungry," said Bertie. "When are you going to feed us again?"

But the man didn't even deign them with a response. He simply walked off and quickly disappeared from view, his feet slapping up what sounded like stone steps.

"He doesn't look like a serial killer," said Elon.

"And how would you know what a serial killer looks like?" said Alec.

"No, I mean, he doesn't give off that serial killer vibe."

"I think the mask tells it all," said Bertie.

"What does it tell?" asked Elon.

"Well, if he really wanted to kill us, in a serial-killer way, I mean, would he be wearing that mask? I don't think so."

'You're absolutely right," said Elon. "That mask tells a story. That mask tells us that he doesn't want to be recognized, and if he really was planning to kill us, he wouldn't be afraid of being recognized, ergo he's not planning to kill us but only going to keep us here for a while and then…" He broke off, and frowned deeply. "Um…"

"And then what?" asked Alec. "Do you really think he abducted us just for the heck of it, and locked us down here just so he could let us go at some point? Think again, bud."

"You don't have to be such a negative Nelly, buddy," said Elon, looking hurt. "I'm just trying to keep the atmosphere light and pleasant, you know, for all our sakes."

"It's always possible he's a shy serial killer, though," said Bertie. "Which would explain the mask. Or maybe he has some sort of facial deformity. The whole cats thing worries me, though. It's just like a serial killer to have some sort of weird cat fixation."

"Oh, my god, don't you see!" said Elon.

"See what?" asked Alec, who was starting to wonder when the comedy double act he was locked up with would stop talking and let him think.

"That's what's going on here! Some kind of secret government experiment. There's us, in here, and the cats, in there, and…" He frowned, and Alec thought he could actually see steam pouring from the poor guy's ears. But then he deflated. "Nah," he said. "I thought I was onto something, but it's gone."

"Look, you keep forgetting that I saw his face," said Alec. "So I don't know why he would wear a mask, since I already know what he looks like. Plus, since I was talking to the guy when I got knocked out, he's got an accomplice who's very handy with a club."

"Food for thought," said Elon, nodding. "You're giving me a lot to work with, chief."

"*W*hat's taking them so long?" asked Harriet irritably.

"I'm sure they're talking to Odelia right now," said Brutus. "And then Odelia will call Chase, and before you know it they will come charging in here and set us all free."

"I'm not so sure," said Clarice. "Harriet is right. They should have been here by now. How long has it been? An hour? Two? Even cats as slow as Max and Dooley should have made the trip and returned by now."

"See?" said Harriet. "Clarice thinks I'm right. And you know Clarice, Brutus. Clarice knows. Clarice is smart. Clarice has been through stuff. So when she says it's taking them too long, she knows what she's talking about."

"I haven't been in this *exact* type of situation, if that's what you're saying," said Clarice.

"No, I don't mean to… I mean… not to make you feel…" She laughed helplessly.

Brutus stared at his mate. He'd never seen Harriet lost for words before, or flustered. Either their current surroundings were having an adverse effect on her, or she was actually feeling intimidated by Clarice. Which was very well possible, of course. After all, he felt intimidated by Clarice practically all of the time and today was no exception.

"I think the only solution will be to claw our way out of this one," said Clarice now, paying no attention to Harriet's weird ramblings. She'd been eyeing the door and now walked over. Harriet and Brutus followed her.

"What do you mean, claw our way out?" asked Brutus.

"What do you think I mean, musclehead?" She pointed to the door. "What do you see?"

"Um… a door?" said Brutus.

"And next to the door?"

"Um… the wall?"

"Oh, God," Clarice groaned. "You wouldn't survive a day in the wild. See those hinges? They're only kept in place with a prayer and a whisper."

"A prayer… and a whisper?" asked Harriet.

"Just give me a paw, will you?" grunted Clarice, and dug a formidable claw into the lowest hinge. Immediately a large chunk of old and rotten cement dropped out.

Brutus exchanged a look of confusion with Harriet. They still didn't see it.

"That door is hinged," said Clarice. "But when we do this…" She removed another thick piece of cement. "It becomes unhinged, see?"

Harriet laughed a nervous little laugh. "I think Clarice is becoming unhinged," she whispered in Brutus's ear.

"I heard that," said Clarice. "Now are you going to give me a paw or what?"

And then Brutus suddenly saw the light. "If those hinges drop out…" he said slowly.

"The door drops out!" said Harriet. "That's brilliant, Clarice."

"Simple physics," said Clarice.

"Shanille! Guys!" Harriet shouted. "Come here a minute, will you?"

In a few words Clarice explained the plan, and soon a dozen cats were working away at those old hinges, scraping off cement and rust and working like good little beavers.

"Now isn't that a sight for sore eyes?" said Clarice as she stood back to admire the work in progress.

"I think your plan is going to work, Clarice," said Brutus.

"No, I mean, have you ever seen cats work together as a team like that before?"

"Um… well, Max and Dooley and Harriet and I often work as a team."

"Yeah, but you're an anomaly. Normally cats are loners. But this… this is beautiful."

"Yeah," Brutus agreed. "It's something, huh?"

"Don't just stand there with your thumb up your butt!" Harriet yelled to Brutus. "Come over here and help us out, will you?!"

Clarice grinned. "You better do as you're told, Brutus. Or there will be hell to pay."

He quickly moved over to where Harriet was digging her claws into the cement. Soon Clarice joined them, and together they made short shrift of the door. And then, suddenly, a wonderful sound: the door was creaking and squeaking, and as Clarice yelled, "Timber!" and all cats got out of the way, the heavy door suddenly dropped down, kicking up some of that ancient and smelly dust. For a moment, no cat spoke. They just stared at the gaping hole. And then they all raced for the exit, and the exodus began.

CHAPTER 28

The door of the van was opened again, and this time Dooley and I were ready to pounce. Only there wasn't anything to pounce on! Instead, it was the same story as before: the contents of the van were poured into the dark hole, and since there was only one way to go, all cats fled in that direction. Soon we landed in that same dank dungeon, only this time there was a big difference: there wasn't a single cat in sight.

"Where did they all go?" asked Dooley.

And then I saw it: the door to the dungeon had collapsed and the road to freedom was open. In the distance I could still see a couple of stragglers, so whatever miracle had caused that sturdy old door to collapse had only happened in the last couple of minutes.

So I said, "Let's go, Dooley. Run!" And run, we did!

Milo, who'd been looking around with a dumb look on his face, said, "Where are my Cat Snax? Where is the Cat Snax team? And where is the plane to Vegas!"

But I wasn't going to hold his paw and escort him out of there. If he wanted to stay put, he was more than welcome.

But since Dooley has a much bigger heart than me, he couldn't allow that to happen, so he said, patiently, "We have to escape, Milo. Or else we'll all be locked up in here and then who knows what they'll do to us."

He gave us a sheepish look. "Um, yeah, I guess you're right. Thanks."

And then we made our way to the exit as one cat, running as fast as our little legs could carry us, which, I can tell you from experience, is pretty darn fast.

And as we raced through the next room in this vast underground lair, I suddenly saw a familiar figure sitting on the floor inside what looked like a man-made cage.

"Hey, Uncle Alec!" I shouted, for it was him. Uncle Alec looked up.

"Max?" he said when he caught sight of me. "Is that you?"

"Don't go anywhere," I said. "We'll go and get help."

"Go and get help! I'll stay here!" he said, sounding like a cuckoo clock.

And then we were tripping up a pair of moss-covered, slick stone stairs.

Once upstairs, Dooley said, "Oh, I've been here before."

And so he had. So now it was his turn to lead the way. We all followed him into a room that had once been inhabitable, then onto a windowsill, and following in Dooley's pawsteps we made the jump down to the ground, narrowly avoiding glass shards, brambles, and decaying pieces of wood, and then we were out. And free at last!

And suddenly I saw three familiar figures exiting the house next door.

Odelia, Chase, and Gran!

*M*arco Lynd had just run down to the corner shop for a six-pack and some frozen pizza and was coming up on the old Buschmann house, his trusty dog Boomer on a tight leash, when a strange sight met his eyes. From inside the house, a sea of cats was emerging, and of course no one was there to stop them.

So he broke into a run. "Gordo!" he shouted. "Gordo!"

Releasing Boomer from his leash, he ran into the house, then straight into the kitchen, where he and Gordo had set up their headquarters.

Of course Gordo was watching a game on the small-screen TV. A swarthy man with thick eyebrows, a bushy beard and a distinct stoop, he barked, "Finally! Where have you been, buddy? I'm starving!" And he reached for the six-pack and cracked one loose.

"The cats!" Marco said, panting. "They're…"

"They're what?"

"They're escaping, you moron!"

Gordo's eyes went wide, and he sprang from his seat, or he would have if he hadn't tipped his chair back, and it now overbalanced and dumped its occupant on the floor, open beer can and all. The beer doused his beard and made a mess, and by the time Marco helped his buddy up and they were out of the kitchen, the cats were long gone.

"Dammit!" Marco cried, and threw his ball cap on the floor for good measure, then stomped on it. Contrary to Gordo, he was thin and rangy, but that didn't mean he was in better shape. And he didn't feel like going off on a wild cat chase.

He searched around for Boomer, and found him whimpering behind a nearby bush, a bloody scratch mark across his nose. "Too many for you to handle, huh, buddy?" he said, patting the dog affectionately. Boomer loved chasing cats, but when faced with a hundred of the damn creatures, he'd clearly had to admit defeat.

Gordo was already on the phone. "Got some bad news for you, sir," he said. "Yeah, the cats escaped. Yeah, all of them." He held the phone away from his ear while a stream of profanities burst from the phone, then held it closer to his ear again. "So what do you want us to do now, sir?"

The response was short and powerful, and Gordo put down his phone.

"Well? What did he say?"

"We have to catch them."

"But we just went and done that!"

"I know. So now we should go and do it again."

"No way!" said Marco, and stomped on his ball cap some more. Only this time a piece of glass had found itself underfoot, and it sneakily sliced into his big toe. And as he was dancing on one leg, he suddenly noticed a woman running in the direction of the house.

It was that nosy reporter. The one who wrote for the *Hampton Cove Gazette*. And when he looked beyond her, he saw she wasn't alone. That damn cop was with her.

CHAPTER 29

The moment Odelia saw a swarm of cats spread out across the road, she halted in her tracks. They'd just walked out of the August house and she'd glanced at the neighboring house, wondering why her intuition suddenly told her to take a closer look, when she suddenly recognized Max, Dooley, Harriet and Brutus!

"It's them!" she yelled. "Chase, Gran! It's the cats!"

And then she was running along the road. The moment she reached her darlings, they jumped into her arms, and buried their faces into her neck.

"Finally," she said. "Finally I found you."

"Or we found you!" Dooley said, and he was right, of course.

Gran had also run up, and Chase, and they all stared at the old house.

"We were held in there," said Max. "In an underground room."

"And Uncle Alec is also in there," Dooley added.

"He's being held in a cage," Max said.

Odelia cut a quick glance to Chase, and he nodded, a grim

set to his face. He took out his phone and called it in. And as he was talking to Dolores, giving her instructions, a white van suddenly emerged from the back of the house, and burst through the rickety old fence, then shot out onto the road. It quickly righted itself, then sped right past them. As it did, Odelia saw two men staring back at her: a bearded one, and a scraggly one.

"That's them!" said Max. "That's the men that abducted us!"

"I'm on it," said Chase, and hurried back to his pickup. He wasted no time firing up the engine and then he was roaring away, in hot pursuit of the suspicious van.

"Let's take a look inside the house," said Odelia. And along with Gran, and her cats, she set foot for the dilapidated old structure.

Max and Dooley led the way, and as they stepped over a bunch of rubble and decaying carpet, then down some slippery stone steps into the basement, it didn't take them long to find the cell where Uncle Alec was locked up, along with two more men.

"Oh, thank God," said Alec. "Once I saw Max and Dooley zipping past, I had a feeling it wouldn't be long before you got here."

"Where are the keys?" asked Odelia.

"No idea. Probably upstairs somewhere. Where's the guard? The bearded giant?"

"Fled," said Odelia curtly. "Chase is chasing him."

"Oh, and he'll get him," said Alec. "Chase always gets his guy."

"And so do we," said Odelia, as she gave her uncle's hand a squeeze through the bars of his cell.

"Really, Alec?" said Gran. "Couldn't you keep out of trouble just this once?"

"Nice to see you, too, ma," said Alec.

"Next time you decide to get yourself kidnapped you should think first."

"Hey, it's not as I chose to get nabbed, ma."

"I'm old, Alec, and my ticker ain't what it used to be. Did you stop to think what all this stress would do to your poor old mother? Huh?"

"I'm sorry, ma," said Alec dutifully. "I'm sorry for allowing myself to get snatched."

"Now go and get me those keys," Gran told Odelia. "So I can give my son a hug, for Christ's sakes."

"Please get my keys, too!" a young man shouted. He had a big zit on the tip of his nose.

"And mine, please, miss!" yelled a bespectacled man in a rumpled brown suit and Burlington socks.

Odelia scaled those stairs as quick as she could, and searched around upstairs. She soon found herself in an old kitchen, the only place that seemed to display recent signs of life, and saw a bunch of rusty old keys lying on the table, next to an ashtray, and a pile of car magazines. She grabbed the keys from the table and hurried back down the stairs, then fumbled with them until she found the right one, and was able to spring her uncle from his prison.

She quickly repeated the procedure with the other two prisoners. One introduced himself as Elon Pope, the lottery winner, and the other as Bertie Balk, the insurance broker with the wife trouble. Both men were over the moon. The story they all told them was the same: they'd found themselves in the vicinity of the Buschmann place, and had been knocked out by a blow to the occipital bone, at which point they must have been dragged downstairs and locked up. To what purpose, they did not know.

"Let's find out if there are more prisoners," said Alec, giving his mother a big hug.

And much to Odelia's surprise, Gran actually got all

teary-eyed. "Thank Odelia, and thank those cats!" she said with a shaky voice when Alec started to thank her. "I was just along for the ride!"

"Thanks, honey," said Alec as he gratefully hugged his niece.

"You're welcome," she said, extremely gratified at how everything had turned out.

"Over here, Odelia!' cried Max, and they all hurried over. Max and the others were in front of a locked door. Behind it, they could hear muffled shouts and pounding.

"It could be more of the bad guys," said Gran as they deliberated their next move.

"So?" said Alec. "I'm more than ready to tackle them if they try any funny business."

"Besides," said Odelia. "Would bad guys lock other bad guys up?"

"Doubtful," Gran agreed.

"Oh, just open the door already!" cried Elon, who couldn't stand the tension.

Odelia tried several keys until one fit, and as the door swung open she was surprised to find herself staring into the faces of… two young boys.

Nicky and Jay.

CHAPTER 30

*T*was so glad to see my human again that I'd almost forgotten about Uncle Alec. Locked downstairs in that dark, dank cell. Luckily Odelia was so clever to find the right key to let him out, and then two other men, and when they found those two kids, I was starting to see this was all part of some bigger thing. After all, who would want to lock up grown men, little kids, and a bunch of cats in the basement of an abandoned house?

There was definitely something nefarious going on, and I couldn't wait to find out what it was.

And so when Odelia went in search of more potential victims, while Gran and Alec took the two boys upstairs, along with the two other prisoners, Dooley, Harriet, Brutus and I decided to join her as she went door to door, looking for a solution to this mystery.

Unfortunately—though I should probably say fortunately —we didn't find more prisoners. What we did find was another staircase, leading even deeper underground.

"I don't know if I want to go down there," said Harriet as we stared into the darkness.

"It does look very spooky," Odelia agreed.

"Maybe we should wait until Chase is back," said Harriet. "He'll know what to do."

"That could take a long time," said Brutus. "Those bad guys could be halfway to Canada by now."

"Chase will catch them," I said. "Didn't you hear what Uncle Alec said? Chase always gets his man."

"Maybe we should wait until the police arrive," said Odelia, then flicked on the Torch app on her phone and let the light play across the wall and those mysterious stairs.

"And what if there are more kids locked up downstairs?" I asked. "Or cats?"

That decided Odelia. She steeled herself, then put her foot on the first step. "I'm going in, you guys. Who's with me?"

"We're right behind you, Odelia," I said, and also took a step down.

"I'm not going," said Harriet. "I'll bet there are rats down there. Big rats. Not nice ones like you see in the movies. I'll bet the rats down there are huge. And really mean."

"I'll protect you, sweetie pie," said Brutus, bravely pushing out his chest.

"Thanks, but no thanks. I'm staying right here. But go if you must."

But since Brutus didn't want to leave his lady love to fend for herself in case there were big nasty rats on this level as well, it was just me and Dooley and Odelia who finally made our way down into the bowels of the earth. Or, as Harriet had pointed out, a potential rat's nest.

We'd reached the last step when the light from Odelia's phone hit a steel door. Next to it was a switch, and when she flipped it, light flooded the stairwell.

"That's much better," I said. "I hate the dark."

Odelia laughed. "But you're a cat, Max. You're supposed to love the dark."

"Well, I don't. Besides, it's a myth that cats can see in the dark. We can't."

"We can see more than humans do, though," said Dooley.

"That doesn't mean I have to love the dark."

His face fell. "You mean… there might be monsters?"

Dooley has a thing about monsters. When he was younger he was always afraid that monsters might be hiding under the bed, and always took a running leap whenever he wanted to jump up on the bed. He also instructed me to stand near the bed when he jumped, in case a monster reached out a tentacle and tried to make a grab for him.

Never once did I see a tentacle, though, or a monster's claw. Still, as I indicated before, I'm not a big fan of the dark either. You never know what's lurking there, right?

Odelia tried several keys, but none of them proved a fit. Then I noticed a little red button right next to the light switch, and directed her attention to it. She pushed it, and the door swung open with a click. The moment we stepped through, lights switched on in the space that lay beyond, and much to my surprise we found ourselves standing inside a very large and industrial-looking room, with all kinds of gleaming machines.

"It looks like… a factory," I said.

"It does," Odelia agreed. And as she walked towards the machine closest to us, she picked up what looked like a stack of plastic casings. She held one up. It was long and transparent. "Oh, my God," said Odelia, her eyes widening. "I think I know what this is!"

We walked further into the room, and she crouched down next to a box standing near another big machine. She picked out an object and triumphantly showed it to us.

"Is that a sausage?" asked Dooley.

"No, it's not," said Odelia with a smile. "It's a saucisse." She gestured to the state-of-the-art equipment. "If I'm not mistaken, this is a meat-processing plant." She walked over to a machine that stretched out along the wall. "See, this is where the meat goes into the machine, and over there is where it's stuffed inside these casings. And at the end of the whole process is a packaging machine, where the finished product is boxed up."

And to prove her point, suddenly a man came walking up to us. He had a small object in his hand. The object was a gun, I now saw, and it was aimed straight at Odelia's chest!

CHAPTER 31

"*M*iss Poole," said the man, whom Odelia recognized as Chris Duffer. "My brother told me you've been snooping around."

"It's over, Mr. Duffer," she said. "The police are on their way. So you better drop that gun and come with me."

"Thank you for the kind invitation, but I'll take my chances." He gestured to the installation. "What a sight, right? This is where the next-generation Duffer was supposed to go into production. In fact this plant should have been up and running already, spitting out thousands of Duffers, but last-minute hitches kept cropping up, baffling my technicians and pushing back the launch. And now, I presume, the whole thing is off."

"So why did you lock up my uncle? And those two little boys? Did they see something they were not supposed to? Did they catch a glimpse of your family's secret formula?"

He gave her a look of incredulity. "You haven't figured it out yet? Shame on you, Miss Poole. I thought you were smarter. But now if you'll excuse me, I better be going."

And before she could stop him, he'd walked off, and

quickly disappeared from view, his footsteps echoing on the concrete floor.

"Stop!" she yelled, and broke into a run. But of course he knew his way around the place a lot better than she did. A door was slammed shut, and when she raced in the direction of the sound, she quickly reached a steel door on the other side of the large space. She yanked open the door and found herself in an underground garage, just in time to see a gray Mercedes drive off, then up a concrete ramp, and vanish from view.

There were several trucks parked down there in what she assumed was a loading dock for the meat processing factory.

Max and Dooley came bursting through the door. "Odelia!" said Max. "You have to see this!"

She followed them back inside, up a few steps into a control room that overlooked the factory floor. There were several consoles from where the production could be monitored, and screens that showed the various stages of the process, from raw meat to finished boxed-up sausage. Everything looked state-of-the-art and brand-new.

Max and Dooley had moved to the far corner, to a small wall safe.

"What do you think is inside?" asked Max. "Money? Jewels? Gold?"

"Something far more valuable," she said, crouching down, and as she put her hand to the safe door handle, she discovered that it was open. Chris Duffer's technicians, whoever they were, must have left it open. She reached inside and took out a small leather-bound notebook. It was old and well-thumbed, and as she leafed through it, saw that it contained notes on how to produce the perfect Duffer, notes probably going back decades, to the first Duffer ever to produce a Duffer. Part of the notes was written in a language she didn't know, but translations had been provided, in the form of a folded document. She unfolded it, and when she read through its contents, gasped in shock.

It contained a list of ingredients for the Duffer:

- Beef 40%
- Pork 30%
- Chicken 20%
- Feline 5%
- Human 1%
- 'Proprietary Duffer Mix' 4%

"Oh, my God," said Odelia, bringing a shocked hand to her face. She reeled, and had to grab the steel door of the small safe to steady herself.

"What is it, Odelia?" asked Dooley.

"The secret ingredients of the Duffer," she said. "One percent human flesh, and five percent cat meat."

Both Max and Dooley gulped. "Oh, my," said Max softly.

In the distance, she heard sirens, and she knew that soon the entire police force of Hampton Cove would descend on the Buschmann house. The Duffers' secret was out…

"Do you think this is a new concept?" asked Max. "Or have they been adding human and cat meat to their famous sausages all this time?"

"I don't know, Max," said Odelia, who couldn't imagine anyone would do such a thing. And to think Gran had feasted from these Duffers, and so had her mom and dad. And then she remembered she'd taken a bite herself, and was suddenly sick to the stomach.

"Oh, look," said Dooley. "The ingredient list for the Proprietary Duffer Mix."

He was pointing to the bottom of the document she'd dropped to the floor.

She nodded absently, still fighting to keep down the contents of her stomach.

"What is MDMA, Max?" asked Dooley, reading from the list.

"What?!" cried Odelia, picking up the document again. And there it was, at the bottom of a long list of harmless ingredients like onion, garlic, wine, vinegar, pepper and salt: MDMA. Also known as XTC.

"So that's why everyone loves those Duffers so much," she muttered.

Against the back wall of the control room a glass-door display fridge had been placed, and when she saw the box of Duffers inside she got up and opened the door with shaking hands, taking one out of the box. She turned it over in her hands. No mention of human or cat meat, of course, or MDMA. How had the Duffers gotten away with this for so long?

She needed fresh air. So she staggered down the few steps from the control room, then into the loading dock and up the ramp. She took out her phone and called Chase.

He picked up at the first ring.

"You'll never know what I just discovered," she said.

"Yes, I caught those guys, thanks for asking," said Chase, sounding energized. Nothing like a good car chase to put the pep in a police officer.

"Do you want to know the secret ingredient of the Duffer?"

"The Duffer? You mean the sausage?"

"Colin and Chris Duffer had a meat processing plant constructed right underneath the Buschmann house, probably figuring no one would ever look there. And do you know why they kidnapped all those cats?"

There was silence at the other end while Chase processed this, then said, in a low voice. "No way…"

"Five percent cat meat and one percent human meat."

"Human meat!"

"*And* a few scoops of MDMA."

"XTC? For real?"

"You better get over here. Oh, and Chris Duffer just made a run for it in a gray Mercedes, so you'll have to track him down, too."

"I'll get on it right away," he promised. "And I'll tell the coroner to get out there, too. If they used human meat, we need to find out who those victims were, and where their remains are buried." He paused. "If there are any remains left, of course."

"This is worse than I imagined, Chase."

"Hang in there, babe. I'm on my way."

Max and Dooley had joined her as they walked up along the ramp.

"I think Alka-Seltzer sales will go through the roof the next couple of days," said Max.

"And a lot of Duffers will be dumped into the garbage disposal," said Dooley.

"Oh, God. You're right, Dooley!" said Odelia, and took out her phone again. This time she called Dan. After she'd told him the story, and given him time to digest it, she said, "Can you put an alert on the website for people to bring all of their Duffers to the police station? I think they'll want to examine them."

"Will do," said Dan. "This is a real horror story you just told me, Odelia," he added, sounding entirely too happy, then promptly hung up to start working on the story.

They'd arrived above ground, where the ramp led straight to a short exit road.

"Clever," she said. The ramp, and as a consequence the exit and entrance to the factory, was well-hidden from the neighboring houses, and if the Duffers were smart about it, they could have limited transportation to the wee hours of the morning, and kept the production facility concealed from nosy neighbors, or the authorities.

"Devious," Max corrected her.

"I think we better get back to the house. This is going to be a long day, you guys."

"And a long night."

She crouched down and held up her hand. Two paws immediately followed suit, and the three of them high-fived. "Well done," she said. "If it hadn't been for you…"

"We didn't do much this time," said Dooley. "We got caught, escaped, then got caught again, and escaped again. The real hero is Clarice. She busted everyone out of that place."

"I'm going to buy her a big slice of…" She grimaced. "Have you ever considered becoming vegetarians?"

Two pairs of cat's eyes stared back at her with abject horror.

"I guess not. Well, I don't know about you, but I'm never eating meat again."

"*Y*uck," said Harriet. "I'm never eating meat again. Ever! Never, never, never!"

"Yeah, you say that now," said Brutus soothingly.

"Cats have to eat meat," said Dooley. "It was on the Discovery Channel. We're carmovores."

"Carnivores," I corrected him.

"That's what I said. Carmovores. Which means we have to eat meat or we get sick and die."

"What about humans?" asked Harriet. "Are they karmaboars, too?"

"Carnivores," I muttered as I let my gaze drift across the backyard.

"I guess. I'm not sure, though," said Dooley.

"Oh, they didn't show *that* on your Discovery Channel, did they?" Harriet said, getting a little worked up. "They didn't say that humans eat cats! And little boys and fat police chiefs!"

"Would you call Uncle Alec fat?" I said.

We all fastened our eyes on Odelia's uncle.

"He is a little pudgy around the middle," said Brutus. "Which is probably why those crooks chose him to be turned into a sausage."

"Come, come, Brutus," I said. "They were never going to turn Uncle Alec into a sausage, or any of those other prisoners, for that matter."

"I know that's what those Duffers told the police, but I don't believe one word they're saying," said Harriet stubbornly.

"Well, I do," I said. "And lab tests bear out their version of the story as well."

"Lab tests can be manipulated."

"Of course they can," I said, not wanting to get into an argument with Harriet when she was like this.

"They should never have moved production of the Duffer from Romania to the US," said Brutus. "If they hadn't, none of this would have happened."

"They would have kept on putting dead Romanians in our sausages!" Harriet said.

Abe Cornwall, the county coroner, had conducted several tests and the Duffers that were sold through the Duffer Store did indeed contain human flesh, but the Duffers had explained they used to buy up bodies from local Romanian morgues and hospitals and used those in their sausages. They also bought up cat cadavers from local vets. In fact they'd established such solid relations with their suppliers over the years they'd even had a town called after them in Grandpa Duffer's birth country. But since Romania had joined the EU, laws had become a lot stricter, and food safety had become an issue, as had the crackdown on rampant corruption. So much so that they'd run out of cadavers at some point—the real reason for the sudden lack of Duffers—and had to find a solution.

So they'd decided to move production to the US and had

made a deal with the Cosa Nostra to take over their dead. Instead of burying their enemies in concrete or dumping them in the East River, the mobsters were to put them on ice and sell them to the Duffers by the pound. And as far as cats was concerned, with seventy-five million cats, the US is the country with the largest cat population in the world, so supply wasn't an issue.

"Is it true they added dog meat to the Chinese Duffer?" asked Brutus.

"It would appear so," I said. "The Chinese were apparently crazy about the Duffer."

"I can't believe the chances they took," said Brutus. "They should have known that people would go to the police when their cats started to go missing."

"Yeah, well, they were under tremendous pressure. They needed fresh Duffers and they needed them quick. Demand was increasing by leaps and bounds but production in Romania had ground to a halt, and if they couldn't deliver soon, their customers might go to the competition and they would have missed a golden opportunity."

"I thought they said every Duffer was handmade? Here in the US?" said Brutus.

"That's the story they told their customers. In actual fact the Duffers have always been made in a factory in Romania, ever since the first Duffer was put inside its casing."

"I still can't believe how anyone could do such a thing," said Harriet.

In the backyard, the party was in full swing, though it wasn't much of a party. After the events of the past week, the entire Poole family had decided to go vegetarian. So no more sausages, or steaks, or ribs. From now on only tofu was on the menu, and lentils. And as Uncle Alec stared morosely into his dish of lentils, he didn't look happy.

The FDA had swept down on Hampton Cove, and the

attention the whole case had garnered had really put the spotlight on our small community. The Duffer was national news, and camera crews roamed the streets, eager to interview Duffer fans.

The scandal had forced Mayor Turner to step down, as well as the secretary of agriculture, and the head of the FDA. In fact the Duffer had caused a lot of heads to roll.

Anti-meat activists and representatives from animal rights organizations had also swept down on Hampton Cove, and our town had become the center of attention. Chief Alec probably would have been forced to step down, too, if he hadn't been one of the victims, and instead had become a popular guest on late-night talk shows. He was even rumored to be the next mayor, though I had my doubts about that.

Uncle Alec loves being chief of police, and once the hubbub died down, as no doubt it would, he'd still be chief, and some whippersnapper would become the new mayor.

Uncle Alec kept pushing his lentils around his plate.

"Delicious, right?" said Marge.

"Oh, yeah," he said, forcing a smile.

"Well, eat up. It's good for you."

"Uh-huh," said Alec, and managed to swallow a whole spoonful without wincing. A definite improvement.

Tex didn't look happy, either, but that was mainly because he'd been relieved from his duties as grill master. Tough to be a grill master when there's nothing to grill. Though he could have tried his hand at the tofu, of course. Difficult to burn tofu. Though I was sure he would give it his best shot.

"I just hope this whole thing goes away soon," said Alec. "Those reporters keep showing up at the office, looking for a quote. I'm all out of quotes!"

"I can't even do my job," said Odelia, munching on a piece

of eggplant. "I'm supposed to chase the story, not be the story. Now they all want to interview me!"

"Well, you did crack the story, honey," said Marge. "Here. Have some quinoa."

"Thanks, Mom," said Odelia without much enthusiasm.

"I'm sure this will all blow over in another week or so," said Chase as he speared a falafel and put it into his mouth. "New scandals pop up all the time, and when they do, the media horde will descend on some other town. Or go back to Washington or New York."

He'd had trouble doing his job, too, as he'd been the one to catch Marco and Gordo and had been declared the hero of the hour, along with Odelia. Their picture had even graced the cover of *Time Magazine* as the crime-fighting couple of the year.

"So they were never going to turn Alec into a sausage?" asked Tex, not for the first time.

"No, they were not," said Odelia. "Marco and Gordo had been hired to provide security. Their orders were to make sure no one discovered the new production line. And if they could catch a cat or two, they earned bonus points. Only they took their job a little too seriously, and knocked out anyone who came within fifteen feet of the house."

"And they figured the more cats they collected, the more money they stood to make," Chase continued, "so they ended up trapping Hampton Cove's entire cat population."

"At least something good came out of it," Gran murmured. She'd been very quiet throughout dinner, barely touching her plate of yellow split peas. Only now did the others notice she'd been playing with a new toy.

"Is that… a smartphone?" asked Marge.

"Oh, you've noticed, have you?" said Gran. "Why, yes, it is, sweet child. Oh, and look what it can do." And before our eyes, she folded it open. It was a foldable smartphone! "And look what happens now," Gran continued, clearly in excellent mood. And she folded it closed again. "Why, it's almost like a miracle, wouldn't you say? A real foldable phone!"

"Where did you get that?" asked Tex, flabbergasted.

"I have my sources," said Gran with a smug smile. "Dick Bernstein gave it to me, okay? He's not as stingy with his money as some people," she added with a pointed look at Tex.

"Dick Bernstein from the senior center?" asked Marge. "But why would he—"

"Because we're going steady, all right? He's always been nuts about me and when I saw him showing off his new phone I told him I'd be his girlfriend if he let me have it."

"You did what?!" cried Marge.

"Ma, that's not very nice of you," said Uncle Alec, but it was obvious his heart wasn't in the fight. The lack of meat probably had sapped him of his strength.

"Who cares? I wanted a phone, and now I got it. See? It folds open like this, and then it closes again like this. It folds open like this, and—"

"Gran, I don't think you should..." Odelia began.

"Shush. You're all jealous of my new phone. So it folds open like this, and then I close it again like this. See? Big screen, small screen. Big screen, small screen. Pretty neat, huh?"

Suddenly there was a light popping sound, and smoke poured out of the phone.

"Eek!" said Gran, and threw the phone into the pot of miso soup.

It made a sizzling sound, and immediately sank to the bottom. And when she fished it out again, and opened it, nothing happened.

"It broke!" she cried. "The damn thing's gone and died on me!"

"Ah, well," said Tex, a beautiful smile spreading across his face. "These things happen."

"It wasn't even mine!" said Gran. "Dick just said I could borrow it, not break it!"

"I'm sure Dick won't mind," said Tex, as he dug into his tofu burger with sudden relish. "In fact I'm sure Dick will be more than happy to buy you another one."

Before anyone could stop her, Gran had picked up the pot of miso soup and was pouring it out over Tex's head. "This is all your fault, Ebenezer Scrooge!"

"This is what happens when humans go vegetarian," said Brutus. "They go nuts."

"Tell me about it," I said as I watched Tex fish a piece of tofu from his collar.

Clarice, who was the real, unsung hero of the events that had rocked our town, jumped gracefully up onto the porch swing. She stuck her nose in the air and sniffed.

"So where's the meat?" she asked. "Where are the sausages? Where are the burger patties? And where's the steak and fries?"

"No steak, no sausages, and no burger patties," said Dooley. "And no steak and fries."

She frowned. "What kind of a barbecue is this? It looks more like a funeral. And why is Tex wearing a soup terrine on his head?"

"I think it's Berghoff, actually," I said.

"It's a vegetarian barbecue, Clarice," Dooley explained.

Clarice hissed her disappointment. "What nonsense!"

"Yeah, they may never eat meat again," said Harriet.

We all lapsed into silence. We hadn't had meat in days, Odelia taking away our regular kibble and soft food and replacing it with a home-made variety consisting of bread, lentils, and vegetables. It was horrible, and I'd never felt so weak and discouraged as I had now. Instead of being feted as heroes, we were being punished. Or at least that's how it felt. And it wasn't just us. The whole town had suddenly gone vegetarian.

Suddenly Clarice hopped down from the swing. "I'm off," she announced curtly.

"Where are you going?" I asked.

"You know me, Max. I'm a strictly meat kind of girl." And she started walking away. We eagerly stared after her, an empty, rumbling sensation in the pit of our stomachs.

She glanced over her shoulder, then cracked us a smile. "All those who want a tasty morsel of meat, follow me."

Without a moment's hesitation, we all jumped off the swing. And then we were chasing after Clarice, who was moving off mightily fast, setting a pretty deft pace.

"Where are we going, Max?" asked Dooley eagerly.

"I have no idea, Dooley, and I don't care."

And I didn't. As long as there was meat at the end of this tunnel, I was on board.

"But what if it's rat, Max?" asked Dooley. "You know how much Clarice likes rat."

I wavered, but only briefly. "Don't be a snob, Dooley," I said. "Rats are animals, too. And they deserve to be eaten just as much as the next turkey or chicken does."

And so off we went, into a bright future that held the only thing that can cheer up a cat, even more so than a cuddle or a pat on the head: a nice, tasty morsel of meat.

Yum!

EXCERPT FROM PURRFECTLY HIDDEN (THE MYSTERIES OF MAX 16)

Prologue

Marge loved these quiet mornings when she had the house all to herself. Tex and Vesta were at the office, and so were Odelia and Chase, and the cats were probably next door having a quiet nap, or out in the backyard wistfully gazing at the flock of birds occupying the big cherry tree. It was a gorgeous morning, and she enjoyed it to the fullest. She'd vacuumed upstairs and downstairs, had put in a load of laundry and was busy in the kitchen, humming along with Dua Lipa's latest hit blasting from the speakers, when suddenly the kitchen tap sputtered and hissed, then gurgled up a small trickle of brown water and promptly died on her.

"Dang it," she muttered as she tried the tap again, with the same result. She stared at the recalcitrant thing for a moment, hands on hips, willing it to work by the sheer force of her willpower, but faucets are tough opponents, and it decided to stay dead instead.

She heaved a deep sigh and called her husband.

"Hey, hon," said Tex as he picked up. "I'm with a patient right now. Can I call you back?"

"It's the kitchen faucet. It's broken."

"Broken, huh? Okay if I take a look at it tonight?"

"Yeah, fine," she said and disconnected. She thought for a moment, then went into the laundry room. It had been conspicuously quiet in there, and she now saw that the machine had stopped mid cycle. And when she opened the tap next to the washer, it was as dead as the one in the kitchen.

Ugh.

She returned to the kitchen and stood thinking for a moment, wondering whether to wait for Tex, but then her eye caught the pet flap Tex had installed in the kitchen door, the one that had cost him a week to put in place and for which he'd needed the help of her brother and Chase to finish, and she picked up her phone again and called her mom.

"I'm busy," said that sprightly old lady. "What do you want?"

"I've got a problem with my plumbing," she said.

"Ask Tex. He's the expert. And wear adult diapers."

"Not my plumbing, ma. The plumbing of the house."

"In that case diapers won't do you any good. And nor will Tex."

"You don't think Tex will be able to fix it?"

"Honey, that husband of yours can't even change a lightbulb without taking down the entire grid. Why don't you call Gwayn Partington? He's a licensed plumber."

"And an expensive one. What about Alec?"

"Forget about it. He's in your husband's league."

"Chase?"

Mom was quiet for a moment. She might not be a great fan of Tex or even her own son Alec, but she had a soft spot for her granddaughter's boyfriend. "Now I wouldn't mind seeing that man in coveralls and a wrench in his hand. Or even without coveralls and a wrench in his hand. Though I'm sure he would do just fine without the wrench."

Both women were silent as they contemplated the image of Chase Kingsley, dressed only in a wrench. Then Marge shook herself. It wasn't right to think of her potential future son-in-law that way. "Is he any good at plumbing, that's what I want to know."

"No idea, honey. But he can always come and clean my pipes, if you know what I mean."

Double ugh.

"Gotta go," said Mom. "Some old coot is yanking my chain. No, the doctor won't see you now, Cooper! You'll have to wait your turn!" she cried, then promptly disconnected.

Next on Marge's list of people to call in a case of an emergency was her daughter Odelia. Before she hired an expensive plumber and spent good money, she needed to exhaust all other—cheaper—possibilities, like any responsible homeowner would.

"Hey, Mom," said Odelia. "What's up?"

"Does Chase know anything about plumbing?"

"Does Chase know anything about plumbing? Well, he is pretty handy."

"Yes, but can he *fix* the plumbing?"

"Honestly? That exact theme never cropped up in any of our conversations."

"But what do you think?"

"I think you better ask Gwayn Partington. He's a licensed plumber."

A deep sigh. "Fine."

What good was it to have three men in the family when none of them could fix the plumbing? Maybe Odelia should have dated a handyman, not a cop. But her daughter was right. Why postpone the inevitable? So she dialed Gwayn Partington's number and was gratified when the man picked up on the first ring.

"Hi, Gwayn. Marge Poole. When do you have time to take a look at my plumbing?"

"I could come over right now, if you want. I had another job lined up but that fell through, so…"

At that moment, her phone warned her that Odelia was trying to reach her, so she said, "One moment please, Gwayn. It's my daughter. Yes, honey?"

"I just called Chase and he says he doesn't know the first thing about plumbing and you better ask an expert if you ever want to enjoy the blessings of running water ever again."

"Thanks, honey," she said, and switched back to Gwayn. "Harrington Street 46. Yes, I'm home."

Ten minutes later Gwayn's van pulled to a stop in front of the house and when she opened the door she felt she'd done the right thing. Gwayn Partington did look amazingly capable, with his blue coveralls and his metal toolkit. At fifty he was pudgy and balding and maybe not the image of male perfection Chase Kingsley was, but at least he would get her faucets all working again, even though he might charge a small fortune.

And as he got down to business in the kitchen, she watched with an admiring eye how he didn't waste time. He fiddled with the tap, then disappeared underneath the sink for a moment, messed around there for a bit, and finally muttered something incomprehensible, took his toolkit and stomped down the stairs and into the basement.

Moments later he was stomping up again, went to grab something from his van and when he returned, soon the sounds of a hammer hitting a brick wall could be heard. Like a regular Thor fighting the demon that had messed up her plumbing, Gwayn swung a mean hammer.

No. This was not a problem Tex could have solved, or Alec, or even Chase.

And as she picked up a copy of *Women's World*, a holler at the front door made her put it down again. "You've got mail, lady!" the new arrival shouted.

She smiled as she got up to meet the mailwoman in the hallway.

"Hey, Bambi," she said as she joined her.

Bambi Wiggins had been their mailwoman for years, and was never too busy for a quick chat. And as she talked to Bambi about the new baby, and Bambi's husband Randi, suddenly a scream rose from the basement. Marge exchanged a look of concern with Bambi, and then both women were hurrying down the stairs. And as they came upon the licensed plumber, who was holding his hammer and chisel and staring at a hole he'd apparently made in the far wall, she asked, "What's wrong, Gwayn?"

The man looked a little greenish, and stood gnawing nervously at the end of his chisel. Already she knew what was going on here. He'd been a little hasty and had made a hole in the wrong place, possibly knocking out a load-bearing wall or a vital part of the house's plumbing system with one ill-advised blow of his hammer. And now, unlike Thor, he was too stunned and embarrassed to admit it.

And as she went in for a closer look, she suddenly halted in her tracks when her gaze fell upon a sight that couldn't possibly be real.

There, sitting and staring at her with its big sockets for eyes, was… a skeleton.

"Oh, my God," Bambi cried. "Marge. You've got a frickin' dead body in your wall!"

And so she had.

Chapter One

We were holding a war meeting in our war room. Well, maybe not a room, per se, but at least a war bush. Dooley, myself, Harriet and Brutus, the four cats that are part of the Poole family feline household, sat ensconced behind the tulip tree at the back of Odelia's backyard for this most important meeting. As befitting a war meeting of the war cabinet in the war bush, there was only one item on the agenda. A very important item.

Mice.

Yes, you read that right. I had called this most urgent and all-important meeting to discuss rodents. You may have seen them scurrying around in your basement or your attic, or even, for the more daring ones, in your kitchen, where they try to steal a piece of cheese, or, let's not limit ourselves to the clichés, a piece of beef or a slice of apple pie. After all, mice will eat almost anything their little hearts desire. As long as it's not too heavy they will carry it between their tiny rodent teeth and make off with it before you realize it's missing.

"We have to do it," said Brutus now, though he didn't seem entirely happy, just like the rest of us.

"I don't know, Brutus," said Harriet. "I don't like the idea of murder. And let's face it, that's what this is: pure and inexcusable homicide."

"Not homicide, though," I said. "Homicide means the murder of a person. A mouse is not a person. It's a rodent, so technically we're talking about rodenticide."

"I don't care what you call it, Max," said Harriet. "It's still a crime against humanity."

"Again, not a crime against humanity. Rodentity, possibly, if that's a word."

"I don't like this, Max," said Dooley, using a favorite

phrase. "I don't want to kill mice. Mice are living creatures, just like the rest of us, and we should let them live in peace."

"Look, I'm all for letting mice live in peace and harmony," I said, "but the fact of the matter is that Odelia has given us an assignment, and we owe it to her to carry it out."

"First off, it wasn't Odelia that gave us the assignment," said Harriet. "It was Tex. And secondly, what can he do if we simply refuse to carry out his orders? Punish us? Hide our food? I don't think he'll do that, you guys. Tex is a doctor, not a monster."

"It wasn't just Tex," I said. "It was Marge, too. And I didn't hear Odelia or Gran or Chase complain when they told us to 'take care of the mouse problem,' did you?"

"If they want the mouse problem taken care of, they should do it themselves," said Harriet stubbornly. "We're cats, not hired assassins."

"It's common knowledge that cats catch mice," I explained.

"No, it's not."

"Yes, it is."

"It isn't!"

"I'm not a killer, Max," said Dooley. "And I don't want anything bad to happen to that sweet little mouse."

"I don't want anything bad to happen to the mouse either!" I said. "But it needs to go."

"So what if some nice Mickey Mouse chose Odelia's basement as its new home?" said Harriet. "Odelia should be happy. She should be glad. She should roll out the welcome mat! A new little friend for us to play with, and a source of joy for the Poole family."

"The mouse has been stealing food," I pointed out.

"Because it's hungry!"

"Maybe Odelia could feed it?" Dooley suggested it. "I

wouldn't mind sharing some of my kibble with a sweet little Mickey Mouse."

"It's not a sweet little Mickey Mouse!" I said. "It's a thief, and if there's one there's probably others."

"I don't see the problem," said Harriet, shaking her head. "I really don't."

"Maybe we should go and talk to the mouse," Brutus now suggested.

"Exactly!" cried Harriet. "If Odelia really wants that mouse to behave, we should talk to the mouse and make it see reason. Tell it to say no to stealing. Reform. But then we also have to talk to Odelia and make her see reason, too. Tell her to adopt the mouse."

I rarely put my paws to my head but I did so now. "Adopt the mouse!" I cried.

"Why not? The Pooles love cats, why can't they learn to love mice, too?"

I leaned in. "Because they specifically told us to get rid of them!"

"We could always ask that sweet little mouse to move," Dooley now suggested. "That way we don't commit mousi-cide, and the Pooles will still be happy."

It seemed like an acceptable compromise, though I could tell Harriet wasn't entirely happy. "I'm still going to have a crack at Odelia and make her see the error of her mouse-hating ways," she said now.

"I think you're wrong," I said, drawing a hissed hush from Brutus. Never tell Harriet she's wrong, he clearly meant to say. But I was getting a little worked up myself.

Harriet drew her nose closer to mine, her eyes like slits. "And when have I ever been wrong about something?" she asked now.

She was going full Terminator on me now, and I almost

expected her to shed her white furry skin and reveal the metal exoskeleton underneath.

"Okay, fine," I said, relenting. "But let's first have a chat with the mouse. And then you can have a crack at Odelia and the others."

"Great," said Harriet, smiling now that she'd gotten her way. "Let me talk to the mouse first, though. I'm sure I can convince it to play ball."

"What ball, Harriet?" asked Dooley, interested.

"Any ball!"

"You would expect that with four cats on the premises this mouse would have chosen another house to make its home," said Brutus.

"Maybe mice are not that smart?" Dooley suggested.

"Oh, I think mice are very smart," said Harriet. "Just look at Jerry. Jerry tricks Tom every time."

We all fell silent. In feline circles mentioning *Tom and Jerry* is considered sacrilege. A cat consistently being bested by a silly little mouse? That show has given cats a bad name. It has made people see us as lazy, dumb, vindictive, vicious and downright nasty. No, Messrs. Hanna and Barbera have a lot to answer for, let me tell you that.

We all moved back into the house, single file, then passed through the pet flap. As usual I was the last one to pass through. There's a silent understanding among the Poole household cats that I always walk through the pet flap last. I'm big-boned, you see, and sometimes the flap refuses to cooperate with my particular bone structure. And as this impedes the free passage of my fellow cats, I'm always last. It was so now, and wouldn't you know it? I got stuck just as I tried to squeeze my midsection through that darn flap.

"Um, you guys?" I now called out. "Can you give a cat a helping paw here, please?"

"Oh, Max, not again!" cried Harriet, sounding exasperated.

"It's not my fault Odelia keeps feeding us primo grub!" I said.

We'd recently been catnapped, Dooley, Harriet, Brutus and I. In fact the entire cat population of Hampton Cove had been catnapped, and after that, to add insult to injury, we'd all been forced to eat vegetarian for a while, on account of the fact that the local populace had discovered they'd been fed cat and even human meat for a long time, an important ingredient in the local delicacy, the Duffer. The Duffer is—or was—a popular sausage, and its creators had taken a few liberties with food safety laws. As a consequence all of Hampton Cove had gone on a veggie kick, which hadn't lasted long.

Also, Vena, who is our veterinarian, and who seems to hate cats so much she likes to poke us with needles and pump us full of something called a vaccine, warned Odelia that cats shouldn't be deprived their daily ration of meat, or else they'll get sick and die.

Odelia had quickly seen the error of her ways and had started feeding us those wholesome nuggets of cat food again, kibble and pouches, and as a consequence I may have overindulged.

Or it could be a malfunction of the pet flap, of course. My money was on the latter.

Dooley took one of my paws, while Brutus took a firm grip on the other, and Harriet assumed the stance of the drill instructor that deep in her heart of hearts she is.

"And... pull!" she screamed. "And pull! And pull. Harder! Put your backs into it!"

"He's not moving!" Brutus cried.

"That's because you're not pulling hard enough, soldier!" she bellowed. "Pull! Pull!"

"I'm pulling as hard as I can!" said Dooley.

"Max, suck in that tummy. Suck it in!" Harriet yelled. "Suck! It! In!"

"Yeah, suck in that flab, Max!" said Brutus, panting from the exertion.

"I'll have you know I don't have any flab," I said haughtily, though it's hard to be haughty when you're stuck in a pet flap and two cats are pulling at your front paws with all of their might. "I'm as lean as that bowl of lean, mean turkey I just gobbled up."

"Less talk, more action!" Harriet was saying. "And pull and pull and pull!"

"I think the problem is that this here darn pet flap has shrunk," I said.

My two benefactors decided to take a short break and let go of my paws.

"Nonsense. You're fat, Max," said Harriet, never one to mince words. "You should go on a diet again."

"Pretty sure it's the flap," I said. "This door is made of wood, and everyone knows wood contracts when it gets cold and wet. It must have contracted. Like, a lot."

"How would this door get wet?" asked Brutus, puzzled.

"It gets really humid at night, Brutus," I pointed out. "Cold and humid."

"The sun has been up for hours. It's warm outside, Max," said Harriet. "So that theory doesn't hold water, I'm afraid. If anything that door should have expanded."

"Someone should go to the other side and push," said Dooley, not taking his eye off the ball, which in this case was me. "One of us could push while the other pulls."

"And how can we go to the other side when Max is blocking the exit?" asked Brutus.

"Maybe we can push from this side," said Harriet. "Make him pop out like a cork."

So the three of them put their paws on my face and started pushing!

"This isn't working," Brutus said after a while. "He's not moving an inch."

It wasn't a pleasant experience, three cats putting their paws on me and poking me in the snoot with all of their might. And Brutus was right. I wasn't budging. On the contrary. I had a feeling I was more stuck now than I was at the start of the proceedings.

And as we all contemplated our next move, I suddenly noticed we had a visitor. A very large mouse had casually strolled up to us and now sat watching the events as they unfolded before its pink whiskered nose.

"So this is what you cats are up to when you're not sleeping or eating or pooping, huh?" said the mouse with a slight grin on its face.

"We do a lot more than sleeping, eating and pooping," said Harriet.

"Oh, sure," said the mouse. "You're also supposed to be chasing me, but I see very little of that going on."

"We're not chasing you because we choose not to chase you," said Harriet. "Because we're all felinists at heart and respect the sanctity of rodent life."

"Yeah, we're vicious mouse hunters," said Brutus, unsheathing a gleaming claw. "The only reason we haven't hunted you down is because we're not into that kind of stuff."

The mouse was studying its own teensy tiny claws, though, clearly not impressed. "You probably don't even know what those claws are for, you big brute."

"I know what these are for," said Brutus, and now showed his fangs, then even managed to make a hissing sound that sounded very menacing and convincing to me.

The mouse produced a slight smile. "You huff and you

puff but you can't even get through that silly little pet door, so forgive me for not being too impressed, fellas."

And with that parting shot, the mouse started back in the direction of the basement stairs, which apparently was its new home. At least according to the Pooles.

"We should probably..." Brutus began, giving Harriet a hesitant look.

"Talk to it!" said Harriet. "We agreed to talk to the mouse so let's talk to the mouse."

Brutus cleared his throat. "Um, mouse? Come back here, will you?"

"That's Mr. Mouse to you, cat," said the mouse, glancing over his shoulder.

"Um, the thing is..." Brutus darted another glance at Harriet, who gave him an encouraging nod. "We've actually been asked to tell you that you're no longer welcome in this house. So if you could please move to some other house that would be really nice."

"Well done," Harriet said with an approving smile. "Very felinistic."

But the mouse laughed. "You're telling me to take a hike? You've got some nerve, cat."

"We happen to live here," said Brutus, stiffening visibly. "And as the co-inhabitants of this house we have every right to ask you to clear out and to clear out right speedily, too."

"Well said, sugar muffin," said Harriet, who seemed to be hardening her stance. Whereas before she'd been a strong defender of rodent rights, she was now eyeing the mouse with a lot more frost than a rodent rights activist should.

"Well, for your information, I like this place, so I'm staying put. And there's nothing you or your dumb chum cat cronies can do about it. So buzz off already, will you?"

"Oh, we'll see about that," said Brutus, finally losing his equanimity. And then he performed the feline equivalent of rolling up his sleeves: he rolled his shoulders and extended his claws. I would have helped him square off against this obnoxious little mouse, but unfortunately I was still stuck in the pet flap, and being stuck has a strangely debilitating effect on one's fighting spirit. Still, he had my most vocal support.

"You don't scare me, cat," said the mouse. "If you want a fight, I'll give you a fight."

"Don't be stupid, mouse," said Harriet, the master diplomat. "We're ten times bigger than you. We can squash you like a bug, and we will if you don't get out of our house."

The mouse wasn't impressed. "It's true that you're bigger than me, cat. But you're also a lot dumber. Besides, much of that size is flab, like your fat red friend who's stuck in that pet flap can tell you, and why should I be scared of a bunch of hairy butterballs? Now if there's nothing more, I've got things to do, mice to see, so cheerio, suckers."

And with these fighting words, he was off, scurrying back to wherever he came from.

He left four cats fuming. Or actually one cat fuming (Brutus), one cat wondering how to get out of the pet flap (yours truly), one cat counting on his digits how much bigger than a mouse a cat could possibly be (Dooley) and one cat looking like the Terminator about to go full metal menace (Harriet).

"Oh, I'll show that little jerk what's what," Harriet hissed. Apparently rodent rights were suddenly the furthest thing from her mind. And as she stalked off in the direction of the basement stairs, Brutus right behind her, I wondered how I was ever going to get out of my pet flap predicament now.

"I think we're actually thirty times bigger than a mouse, Max, or maybe even more. What do you think?"

"I think I want to get out of here," I said.

"I think the situation will take care of itself."

"You mean the mouse situation?"

"No, your situation. If you simply stay stuck for a while and don't eat, you'll automatically get thinner and get unstuck before you know it."

And having delivered this message of hope, he plunked down on his haunches, and gave me a smile, entirely ready to keep me company while I accomplished this rare feat.

"It will take me days to slim down and get unstuck, though," I said, pointing out the fatal flaw in his reasoning.

"I don't think so. A lot of weight gain is fluids," said Dooley. "So the key is to get dehydrated." He nodded wisely. "You need to sweat, Max, and sweat a lot. And then all of that extra weight will simply melt away."

And to show me he wasn't all talk and no action, he got up, jumped on top of the kitchen table, flicked the thermostat to Maximum, and jumped back down again.

"There," he said, satisfied with a job well done. "It's going to turn into a sauna in here and you'll be free before you know it." He gave me a reassuring pat on the head.

Odd, then, that I wasn't entirely reassured.

Chapter Two

Over at the office, Tex was watering his spider plant while listening to the radio. He'd turned up the volume, as the song that was playing happened to be one of his favorites. It was a golden oldie from that old master of melody Elton John. And as he sang the lyrics, exercising the old larynx, he suddenly realized how much he actually liked to sing.

"Humpty Dumpty doo wah doo wah," he warbled softly.

The spider plant was one of his favorites. He'd gotten it as a present from his daughter a couple of years ago, after she'd been in to see him about a suspicious mole that had developed on the back of her hand, and had told him his office looked dark and gloomy and could use sprucing up. In the week that followed she'd assumed the role of head of the sprucing-up committee and had redesigned his office, making it lighter and airier.

It had been her idea to put in the skylight, and to throw out the old rug that had developed a strange odor after years of use. She'd had the original wood floor sanded and refinished so it shone when the sun cast its golden rays through the new skylight, and as a finishing touch had thrown out his old furniture and replaced it with a nice and modern-looking desk and chair. Now the office didn't look like it belonged to a nineteenth-century sawbones but a modern young physician hip with the times.

"Doo wah doo wah," he sang, louder now that he decided that he had a pretty great singing voice. "Doo wah doo wee wee weeh…"

On the other side of the door, Vesta was watching a YouTube video on her phone. There were no patients in the waiting room, and no patients in with Tex either, so she had all the time in the world. But this video was something else. And as she watched, suddenly a horrible noise intruded on her viewing pleasure. It sounded like a cross between the howl of a wolf and the yowl of a cat in heat. It took her a while to trace the source of the sound, and when she had, she got up and marched over to the door.

Without knocking, she opened it and stuck her head in.

"Tex? Are you all right?" she asked, showing a solicitude she rarely displayed when dealing with her son-in-law.

"I'm fine," said Tex, looking up from watering his plant. "Why?"

She shook her head. "The weirdest thing. I thought I heard someone being mangled by a timber wolf but now it stopped."

"You're imagining things, Vesta, cause I heard nothing."

"Yeah, that must be it," she murmured, then made to close the door, only to push it open again. "Say, have you ever considered we may be about to be annihilated, Tex?"

"Mh?" he said, looking up from plucking something from his precious plant.

"The coming apocalypse," she explained. "I was just watching a great video about the coming apocalypse and what we should do to get ready for when it comes."

"What apocalypse?" he asked, getting up and staring at whatever he'd plucked from his plant.

"The one that's about to start. There's a nuclear holocaust about to happen, Tex, or hadn't you noticed?"

"No, actually I hadn't. What nuclear holocaust?"

"Well, it only stands to reason that with so many nuclear weapons in the world someone is gonna launch one any second now, and that someone may be a rogue agent, or it may be a rogue nation, or it may be a rogue organization. Something rogue at any rate. And then there's the tsunamis that are about to rock our world, not to mention the volcanoes that are about to go active, and the rising oceans. We need to get ready, Tex. It's imperative we build ourselves a bunker and store it with enough food to survive this thing."

He gave her a strange look. "Vesta, there's not going to be a nuclear holocaust. The people in charge will never let that happen. And as far as those oceans and those volcanoes are concerned, I'm sure it will all be fine."

"All be fine! You sound like those animals that stick their heads in the sand! Kangaroos? No, ostriches." She pointed a finger at him. "You, Tex, are an ostrich, and it's because of ostriches that things are quickly going to hell in a handbasket."

"Uh-huh," he said, not sounding all that interested. "What do you think these are?" he asked, staring at his own finger like the ding-dong he was. "Is that a bug, you think, or a fungus?"

"Oh, you're a fungus, Tex," she said, and slammed the door shut.

It didn't matter. Even though Tex was a lost cause, that didn't mean she couldn't take matters into her own hands. Wasn't that always the case, though? Didn't it always come down to simple, honest, hard-working women to get the job done?

So she got behind her desk, took pen and paper in hand, and started scribbling down a list of things she needed to get cracking on to survive this coming nuclear winter.

"It's been in there an awfully long time," said Uncle Alec, staring at the skeleton.

"And how long is an awfully long time?" asked Odelia. "In your expert opinion?"

"Heck, honey, I'm just a cop, not a coroner. So I have absolutely no idea."

"I'll bet it's been in there a thousand years," said Marge. "Look at the state it's in."

"I doubt it's been a thousand years, though, Marge," said Chase. "This house isn't a thousand years old."

"So what? It could have been there from way before this house was ever built."

"Impossible, mom," said Odelia. "It's in the wall, so it was put there after the house was built."

"Oh," said Marge. "You think?"

"I'm not an expert either, but yeah, that's what I think."

"Abe should be here any minute now," said Alec, checking his watch. "We'll know more when he arrives."

Abe Cornwall was the county coroner, and as such more

qualified than any of the small band of onlookers who now stood gathered around the skeleton, staring at it as if hoping it would magically reveal its secrets somehow.

"I still don't have water," Marge pointed out. Her initial shock had worn off.

Odelia placed a hand on her mother's shoulder. "Don't worry, mom. As soon as the body is taken out, I'm sure the plumber will be able to get the water running again."

"Yeah, but the laundry still needs to be done, and I need to cook, and I wanted to mop the floors—though now with all these people running in and out of the basement I guess it's not much use anyway."

"If you want you and Dad and Gran can eat at ours tonight."

"Thanks," said Marge. "But what about showers tomorrow morning?"

"You can take a shower at ours, as well."

"Thanks, sweetie," said Marge, biting her lip nervously.

"So Gwayn took a whack at this wall and this skeleton popped up," said Alec, jotting down a couple of notes.

"Yeah, Gwayn figured there was an issue with the connection to the water main—a leak maybe—so he wanted to take a closer look before he called in the people from the water company. And that's when this old skeleton suddenly popped up," said Marge.

Gwayn Partington had gone home already. Or, as was more likely, to his favorite bar.

"Clothes are mostly gone, too," said Alec. "Though they look like a man's clothes to me."

The skeleton had a few rags draped around itself. It was hard to see what they'd been, though, in spite of what Odelia's uncle said. Everything looked old and ragged.

"Look, just get it out of here, will you?" said Marge. "So I can call Gwayn and he can fix my plumbing and I have water again." And with these words she moved up the stairs.

"So how long do you really think it's been there, Uncle Alec?" asked Odelia.

"Hard to say, sweetie. These houses were built in the fifties, so it has to be less than that, and bodies take a little while to turn into skeletons, so it can't be recent, either. But like I said, it's up to the experts to tell us the age of the body, or how it died."

"And how it got stuck inside this wall," Chase added.

"But it didn't get stuck inside the wall, did it?" said Odelia. "Someone put it there."

Alec moved a little closer and stuck his head in to look up. "Yeah, doesn't look like a chimney or anything, so it's definitely not some wannabe Santa who got stuck."

"Ha ha," said Odelia. "Very funny."

"No, it happens," said Alec, retracting his head. "I once heard about a case where a guy went missing. Years later a house in the same neighborhood was sold and when the builders came in to do some remodeling they found a body stuck inside the old chimney. Turns out he'd been burgling the house and had gotten stuck and died."

"You know what this means, right?" said Odelia.

"What?"

"This is a murder case."

"A murder case!" said Alec.

"Of course. What else could it be?"

"Anything! A very elaborate suicide. An accident. Um…"

"It's murder, and whoever put this poor person in there managed to get away with it for all this time."

"Oh, don't tell me you think we should…" Alec began.

"Investigate who killed him or her? Of course. It doesn't matter if it happened yesterday or fifty years ago, we need to get to the bottom of this."

"But—"

"There's people out there who lost a brother, a sister or a mother or a father. And who never had closure. People who want to know what happened, and who deserve answers, and to see justice done. And the murderer is probably still out there, happy they got away with it. Well, I would like you to promise me you're not going to let that happen. That you're going to do whatever it takes to bring this person to justice."

ABOUT NIC

Nic Saint is the pen name for writing couple Nick and Nicole Saint. They've penned novels in the romance, cat sleuth, middle grade, suspense, comedy and cozy mystery genres. Nicole has a background in accounting and Nick in political science and before being struck by the writing bug the Saints worked odd jobs around the world (including massage therapist in Mexico, gardener in Italy, restaurant manager in India, and Berlitz teacher in Belgium).

When they're not writing they enjoy Christmas-themed Hallmark movies (whether it's Christmas or not), all manner of pastry, comic books, a daily dose of yoga (to limber up those limbs), and spoiling their big red tomcat Tommy.

www.nicsaint.com

Nora Steel

Murder Retreat

The Kellys

Murder Motel

Death in Suburbia

Emily Stone

Murder at the Art Class

Washington & Jefferson

First Shot

Alice Whitehouse

Spooky Times

Spooky Trills

Spooky End

Spooky Spells

Ghosts of London

Between a Ghost and a Spooky Place

Public Ghost Number One

Ghost Save the Queen

Box Set 1 (Books 1-3)

A Tale of Two Harrys

Ghost of Girlband Past

Ghostlier Things

Charleneland

Deadly Ride

Final Ride

Neighborhood Witch Committee

Witchy Start

Witchy Worries

Witchy Wishes

Saffron Diffley

Crime and Retribution

Vice and Verdict

Felonies and Penalties (Saffron Diffley Short 1)

The B-Team

Once Upon a Spy

Tate-à-Tate

Enemy of the Tates

Ghosts vs. Spies

The Ghost Who Came in from the Cold

Witchy Fingers

Witchy Trouble

Witchy Hexations

Witchy Possessions

Witchy Riches

Box Set 1 (Books 1-4)

The Mysteries of Bell & Whitehouse

One Spoonful of Trouble

Two Scoops of Murder

Three Shots of Disaster

Box Set 1 (Books 1-3)

A Twist of Wraith

A Touch of Ghost

A Clash of Spooks

Box Set 2 (Books 4-6)

The Stuffing of Nightmares

A Breath of Dead Air

An Act of Hodd

Box Set 3 (Books 7-9)

A Game of Dons

Standalone Novels

When in Bruges

The Whiskered Spy

ThrillFix

Homejacking

The Eighth Billionaire

The Wrong Woman

Made in the USA
San Bernardino, CA
04 August 2020